THE
HOMECOMING
and other stories

ALSO BY SRI M

On Meditation: Finding Infinite Bliss and Power Within

THE
HOMECOMING
and other stories

SRI M

PENGUIN BOOKS

An imprint of Penguin Random House

PENGUIN BOOKS

USA | Canada | UK | Ireland | Australia
New Zealand | India | South Africa | China

Penguin Books is part of the Penguin Random House group of companies
whose addresses can be found at global.penguinrandomhouse.com

Published by Penguin Random House India Pvt. Ltd
7th Floor, Infinity Tower C, DLF Cyber City,
Gurgaon 122 002, Haryana, India

First published in Penguin Books by Penguin Random House India 2020

ISBN 9780143447528

Typeset in Adobe Caslon Pro by Manipal Technologies Limited, Manipal
Printed at Replika Press Pvt. Ltd, India

www.penguin.co.in

Contents

Death of a Builder

He was a hard worker. Patiently and diligently, he toiled round the clock with one-pointed attention, oblivious to his surroundings, building his own little private hideout, for on it depended his glorious future.

At the moment, he was a person of no importance, an unfortunate, substandard, clumsy creature, pale and ugly. But he knew, that would soon be a thing of the past, for he was no longer a child.

Like all the members of his family for generations, the first sign that heralded the onset of maturity in his case too was the spontaneous longing to rise high above his station. To be able to fly like an angel through the heavens, to go out into the beautiful wide world and flirt with the sweet-scented flowers as they danced to the cool breeze. He was still grovelling in the dirt, but his eyes had fastened themselves to the twinkling stars wide above.

No one had to tell him how to go about fulfilling his ambition. No one had to tell his father his father either, or his grandfather. Just as it had happened to them, the entire project worked out to the last detail was now unfolding before his inner eye on this fine sunny morning. He was thrilled to discover that the special fluid which had started to ooze out of his body was all he needed as a raw material. Instantly, he set himself to the task of building his cell.

First, he attached himself to the under portion of his favourite bush. Then he drew thin but surprisingly tough glistening strands out of the sticky, magic substance that his body exuded and proceeded to weave it carefully around him into a spheroidal, single room.

When he had finished working, the windowless, doorless meditation chamber he had built for himself filament by filament, out of his own blood, hung cucumber-like from under the tree, with him safe and secure inside it, protected from the harsh sun, the rains and the fierce wind.

He had nothing more to do than to relax. In the pitch darkness, free from all distraction, he could meditate and contemplate the delightful world that would be his when he emerged after his period of retreat. A new and beautiful winged creature, able to fly freely and go where he pleased, no more a worm.

It was while he was immersed in blissful visions that they came, the Homo sapiens, to plunder and to exploit.

He was rudely shaken out of his trance as they briskly plucked out hundreds of these hanging habitats, complete with their occupants inside, and took them away to a hot, stuffy room.

There, with a song of delight on their lips, they plunged the whole lot into a huge cauldron of boiling water. In one brief moment of inexpressible agony, his dreams were shattered, and his very life snuffed out.

Out of the spoils of the mass slaughter they gathered pure silk. They unwound and separated the glistening strands he had spun and, after treating them in special baths, rolled them up into neat balls of silk-thread, ready for the weaver's loom.

From this were made beautiful, flowing lengths of shimmering silk so dear to the hearts of the cultured and the refined—it was sent to drape gods and goddesses who had little time for the humble, the hard-working, the lowest of the low.

The Porter

The well-built, curly haired young man of medium height, dressed in blue jeans, red T-shirt and brown ankle boots, carried only one piece of luggage—a small-sized, glossy black Ecolac briefcase.

Krishna, with his twenty years of experience as a licensed porter at the Bengaluru City railway station and given to watching all kinds of people with all kinds of luggage, noticed that not once since he had entered the platform had the young man put down the briefcase. Unusual, because from the way he carried it there was little doubt in Krishna's mind that the briefcase, though small, might be heavy.

'Gold ornaments, may be even gold biscuits,' Krishna said to himself. He had carried what he guessed was gold many times. Bangaru Chetty, the well-known jeweller, always engaged him to carry his luggage. Chetty trusted him.

Trust. A lot of people trusted him but what had he gained? Nothing.

He rubbed his fingers across the brass badge pinned to his red T-shirt which proclaimed that he was a licensed porter, licensed to carry other people's luggage all his life, while he himself possessed nothing other than life's burdens: a heavy load which he knew no one else would care to share. So much for trust and honesty.

Krishna wasn't the type who coveted someone else's property but under the prevailing circumstances, in sheer desperation, he was willing to deviate from the principled life he had led thus far. What had his high principles given him, as his wife once said, 'except poverty, misfortune and eternal sorrow?'

'Just this once,' he said to himself. 'Let me give it a try. Must be a smuggler. The loss would be nothing to him.'

The station was crowded. Armed policemen stood outside a special coach of the Chennai Mail, guarding some politician, an ex-minister of Tamil Nadu who, for some strange reason, had decided not to spend the taxpayer's money flying and go by train.

Krishna steadied his nerves with great effort and walked up to the young man with the briefcase who was standing outside the second-class sleeper coach adjoining the minister's VIP coach. Hardly ten minutes left for the train to start and he was still outside. Perhaps waiting for someone.

'Porter, sir?' said Krishna and gestured towards the briefcase.

The young man said, 'No,' and turned his face away.

Under normal circumstances, Krishna would have gone and found another traveller but that day he just stood beside the news-stand nearby absorbed in his own thoughts.

'Krishna,' he said to himself 'You are not made out for that kind of stuff, see? You certainly can't snatch the briefcase and run. Crime is not your cup of tea. You can't do it. So, suffer. Be an honest man . . .'

The young man walked into bogie number S3, just five minutes before 10.30 p.m., the scheduled departure time. Krishna saw him occupy the window seat on the platform side and immediately afterwards walk out of the train empty-handed and head towards the canteen, quite a distance from his compartment.

Puzzled, Krishna watched as the minutes ticked by on the dial of the large station clock.

The guard whistled and waved the flag, the lights turned green and the announcer made the departure of the train known.

The train began to move. For a moment, Krishna stood rooted to the spot before breaking into a run. 'Now or never.'

He climbed into the compartment and ran down the aisle until he came to the seat he had seen the young man occupy. He found the briefcase lying on the upper berth.

'Got it, sir!' he shouted in Kannada, pressing his face to the window, as if speaking to someone outside. He then picked up the briefcase and ran outside. As he passed the old, grey-haired lady who sat on the opposite seat, he said loudly, 'Wrong train. Poor man.'

He continued to run until he reached the last one of the linked sleeper-class compartments. By now the train had gathered speed and had moved out of the platform. The ticket collector was at the other end and no one else seemed to give any serious attention to his movements. Taking advantage, Krishna jumped out of the train, adjusting his gait to avoid falling. He found himself in a lonely spot close to a water tank. Nearby stood an abandoned locomotive shed.

A fluorescent street light a few feet away shed its light on the surroundings. The train had now disappeared into the darkness.

He stood still for a while, briefcase in his hand, taking stock of the situation. It was clear that he couldn't walk out of there or go home carrying an elegant, new briefcase. He would have to transfer the contents into his old worn-out airbag in which he carried his uniform and lunch-box every morning when he came to the station. But first he had to get it from the cupboard in the second-class retiring room.

Krishna looked around. There was no one in sight. He entered the abandoned shed. A little bit of light filtered in from the broken roof and wild bushes grew all over. He hid the briefcase in a corner near a lantana bush and stepped out. There was no one around.

Suppressing his excitement with great effort, he slowly walked back to the platform and entered the retiring room as nonchalantly as he could manage, hoping no one would ask him inconvenient questions.

Just outside the retiring room stood Ramappa, the attendant.

'What, Krishna, waiting for the 11.30 arrival or going home?'

'Going home,' said Krishna. 'Not feeling well.'

He collected the bag from the shelf and walked back to the shed to collect the briefcase, which was locked, just as he had expected it to be. He decided to break it open after going home, if it could somehow be fitted into the bag. Luckily it did. In fact, to his relief, it fit in quite easily.

Carrying the bag, he walked towards his tiny, two-room tenement; one of the rows of forty such structures built by the Karnataka Slum Development Board, two kilometres away from the railway station, facing the railway tracks.

The bag with the briefcase inside was indeed heavy, just as he had thought it would be.

As he walked he felt guilty of having committed a terrible crime. Krishna was sure no one suspected anything but that was not the point. Never before had he acted this way.

He debated the idea of walking back to the station and keeping the bag at the Railway Police Station. But he thought of his sick wife coughing blood and his only daughter, the apple of his eye, who was still to be married off. How many months since he had bought her a new set of clothes? How was he going to find a husband for his dear Meenakshi without paying dowry?

He felt the money in his pocket. Just about fifty rupees. The daily average. Barely enough for food.

'No. Just this once. Never again.'

The briefcase was as heavy as one of Bangaru Chetty's bags. 'The fellow must be a smuggler who has access to more of whatever is inside, but for me, for porter Krishna, this is my only chance. God, please forgive me if I am doing wrong. I know you will.'

He began to walk faster.

Krishna reached his house at around 11.30 p.m. As usual the front door was not locked. It was merely shut.

He pushed open the door and went in. Apart from the tiny kitchen there were only two rooms. In one of them was an old hand-operating sewing machine his nineteen-year-old daughter used to earn a few rupees doing simple stitching and mending jobs for the neighbours. She had fallen asleep on a floor mat, waiting for him. Beside her was his dinner: Ragi balls, beans curry and tamarind chutney.

Meenakshi was smiling in her sleep. Her dream world was perhaps happier than the real world he had brought her into. Tears came rolling down his eyes as he saw her torn skirt, plastic bangles and imitation gold earrings. Perhaps it would all change now. How lovely she would look with real gold ornaments!

He was hungry but decided to eat later. First, he had to open the briefcase and he had better do it without waking them up. There was no light in the other room where Ambuja, his wife, seemed to be sleeping soundly, thanks to the sleeping tablets he had managed to get her in the morning.

Carrying the briefcase, he tiptoed into the tiny kitchen. The electric light wasn't working because the bulb had popped. He lit the kerosene lamp, softly pushed the door shut and sat on the floor. Holding the briefcase in his lap he examined the locks, trying to figure out the best way to pry them open with the least noise.

That was when he heard the peculiar ticking sound coming from inside the briefcase. What happened next took only a split second. A fire-orange, dazzling flash, followed by an ear-splitting blast! Krishna couldn't complete the scream that rose in his throat.

The same night, just as the train moved out of the station, the young man emerged from the canteen, walked up to the public telephone booth and dialled his boss's number.

'Okay sir, all done. Too much security for the minister, sir. Didn't want to risk getting caught, so planted the briefcase in the next compartment. Range more than enough, sir.'

'Thank you, goodbye,' said the man on the other side and hung up. Then with a smile on his lips, he poured himself a peg of Old Monk rum and drank it up straight, celebrating in advance the death of Enemy Number One. The state's ex-home minister and founder-chairman of the National Committee for Combined Action Against Terrorism (NCCAAT) would be blown to shreds in an hour or so. A warning to all who opposed the revolution. Many others would die as well. But so what?

The next day's media reports mentioned a mysterious midnight explosion in a colony of the Karnataka Slum Development Board, two kilometres from the city railway station, which caused extensive damage over a wide area and resulted in the death of over fifty people. The police suspected that the blast was caused by a powerful time-bomb and investigations were underway to find out why that particular area had been targeted and who was responsible for it.

Krishna never again had to carry either anybody's luggage or his own burdens. The only thing left of his body was his right arm from the elbow downwards.

The Guru's Last Day

There was this air of utmost expectancy, almost desperate, as if everything depended on his appearance.

The stage was all set; the usual paraphernalia, soft, digital music of the flute, the semi-circular stage bedecked with bright orange and golden yellow flowers. The costly Persian carpet in the centre on which stood a red, velvet-cushioned golden throne.

He would, at any time now, make a dramatic entrance from the small white curtained entrance on the side of the otherwise deep blue backdrop.

A thousand-strong crowd sat, waiting as if all their life's desires hinged on the appearance of the great one. They were waiting to feast their eyes and hear the sacred words uttered.

Men and women, young and old, Indians and non-Indians, damsels and modern knights, all in search of the Holy Grail, dark-haired, brown-haired and blonde. Hippy types and proper gentlemen, disabled ones hoping to be healed, some in wheelchairs, a few monks in saffron clothes, the official videographers and, of course, the disciples of the great one, white-clad men and women hurrying up and down, making sure everything was in order. Close to the stage stood a couple of armed security men, bouncers you could call them, over six feet tall and muscles rippling under their brown safari suits.

Perfect silence as if it was a congregation of the dumb, broken only by the gentle music of the flute, appropriate to the occasion, mellifluous, hypnotic.

The white silk curtain on the left side was pulled aside electronically. The music shut off abruptly and so entered the great one—not so great in physical stature—clad in a pure white silk gown starting at the neck and going down all the way to the ankles; a dark-complexioned man, hardly five feet four inches, but undoubtedly charismatic with a clean-shaven, almost handsome face, liberally doused with moisturizer, glistening and abundant flowing hair that reached his shoulders, dyed coal black for he was over sixty. Large dark and sharp eyes, darting in all directions, surveying the crowd closely. After all, there had been an attempt on his life just two weeks ago.

An audible gasp swept through most of the crowd whose eyes were one-pointedly glued to the great Guru.

With hands folded in namaste, many of the devotees chanted 'Jai Guru Maharaj' in chorus.

Someone shouted, 'Oh my God, my all.'

A couple of women fainted. One screamed 'O Lord, O Lord' in a shrill voice.

A young man in the third row stood up and whirled like a dervish. A low whisper filled the air. The white-clad disciples went about trying to keep everyone quiet. The dancing man was made to sit down and the screaming woman was silenced.

Bare-footed Guru Maharaj with his tiny, almost feminine feet, walked softly up to the throne and sat down. Two sturdy, muscular disciples in white came and stood on either side of the throne.

Two blondes in white came up to the stage from either side. One garlanded his neck with jasmine flowers and the other placed a fully blossomed lotus at his feet, which rested on a red velvet foot stool. Then they withdrew discretely.

When Guru Maharaj spoke, God spoke. The slightly feminine voice rang clear. The hidden microphone he was wired up with was of the highest quality.

'Dear ones, I am here this evening to tell you the good news that there is hope for all. All you need to do is to keep me in your heart and make no other effort.

'Close your eyes and see me smiling inside the sanctum sanctorum of your hearts. Breathe in and out wholly. Chant a long Om in an even tone and relax. Om . . .'

The chanting of the Om filled the air. Most of the audience, except the journalists and a few politicians seated in chairs in the front row, were absorbed in the exercise, eyes closed. Guru Maharaj's eyes remained open too and so were those of the bodyguards who alertly scanned the premises.

Peaceful smiles appeared on their faces. Some swayed gently to and fro and others sat ramrod straight. They certainly were in a tranquil and blissful mood. The soft digital music came back softer than before. Around half an hour of unalloyed bliss. The gentle breeze of a November evening and the crescent moon that rose over the lawns added to the effect.

The spacious lawns of Shanti Vihar—home of peace, located in Chhatarpur—transformed into heaven for the devotees.

With a drop of his hands and a loud 'Hari Om', Guru Maharaj brought them back to the earth. While they were still coming back from the pinnacle of peace, their God, Guru Maharaj, quickly stood up and, accompanied by the bodyguards, disappeared though the door he had entered.

Once more the crowd prostrated and the sound of 'Jai Guru Maharaj' rose from a thousand throats. Some of the devotees were even seen sobbing uncontrollably.

* * *

One minister and another senior politician were led by the volunteers to the interview room in front of the palatial residence of Guru Maharaj. The minister discussed how his political rival was now creating trouble for him and sought blessings to win the upcoming election.

'I am with you,' said Guru Maharaj. 'Nothing to fear.' He left clutching the lotus given by the holy man. He would keep it in his puja room until it faded and dried.

The other politician had some serious questions on spiritual life. He got answers which were to his satisfaction and went back beaming.

Dr Ramakant, Guru Maharaj's personal secretary as well as his personal physician, the handsome, fifty-five five-year-old ex-Army doctor entered the room.

'No more personal interviews scheduled for today Guru Maharaj,' he said. 'I think you should get some rest. You just flew in this morning from Atlanta.'

'I don't need to rest but good, I can be in solitude until I go to sleep. So, I wanted to ask you, how is the old devotee Jayantilal doing?'

'Still in the ICU in a coma, Guru Maharaj.'

'Any relatives that turned up to see him?'

'No, Guru Maharaj. After they learnt that he has willed all his assets and property to the Shanti Trust, not one has turned up. Heard his son was contemplating legal proceedings against the Trust saying his father was made to sign the papers under stress.'

'Who is in charge of the ICU?'

'Dr Mandira.'

'Send her over tomorrow morning. I would like to talk to her. Jayantilal's soul has come to me several times and begged to be freed so that he can seek refuge in me. To free him from the body would be an act of kindness and I would like to know what Dr Mandira can do to hasten the process.'

For a second, Dr Ramakant's thoughts trailed off. Hadn't he heard this twice before? Then he broke the chain of thought that had momentarily occupied his mind and spoke.

'Will talk to Dr Mandira and let you know when I come back to give you the insulin shot.'

'Okay, see you then.'

* * *

Dr Ramakant walked out of the room and proceeded to his residence. His brain still abuzz with thoughts he could not curb. Hatred for this man who called himself Guru Maharaj drowned all other reason.

***

Guru Maharaj had a light dinner of moong dal kichadi and yogurt brought to him from the private kitchen, had a glass of hot milk and sat in his rocking chair looking out of the window at the night sky with a beautiful crescent moon playing hide and seek among the clouds.

***

Outside, the blonde Hollywood star, Cathy, was having a conversation in the little guest room allotted to her, with a friend from Australia.

She told her how two years ago, before she had met Guru Maharaj for the first time, she had not slept for six months. Even sedatives didn't help. Guru Maharaj had blessed her and given her some Ayurvedic tablets to be taken for a month and told her to meditate on his image in her heart and chant 'Jai Guru Maharaj'. She didn't even need the tablets now. She just had to chant 'Jai Guru Maharaj' silently and think of him and she would fall asleep instantly.

After her friend said goodnight, that was precisely what Cathy did. She stretched herself on her bed, visualized Guru Maharaj in her heart, chanted her mantra and fell asleep in a few minutes.

***

Guru Maharaj wasn't as lucky. Unable to chant his own name, he needed a sleeping tablet to be blessed with blissful sleep. But he would wait for the insulin shot before taking his Ambien 5 mg. He had been a diabetic for ten years now and needed a shot of insulin every morning and evening.

Dr Ramakant would come soon and perhaps he would have some good news about Jayantilal and when he would finally be declared dead.

* * *

Dr Ramakant shut the door and lowered himself on to the armchair by the window. From the window he could see the palatial residence of Guru Maharaj. He closed his eyes and his thoughts went back to the accursed day he had first met him. Back then, he had thought that it was the most blessed day of his life.

He was then a young major working in the Army Medical Corps and had, for many years, been reading books on Indian philosophy, mysticism and yoga. Impressed by an article he had read in a newspaper about Guru Maharaj, and convinced that this man would probably be the right Guru to initiate him into the spiritual life, he had somehow managed to locate him. Those were the days when the Guru Maharaj was not so well-known.

His wife had accompanied him reluctantly to the small ashram in Haridwar, more out of curiosity, for she wasn't interested in either religion or philosophy, and was a neurosurgeon who prided herself on being an atheist.

He had fallen for him on that very first meeting. He seemed so caring, peaceful, and so insightful. Guru Maharaj seemed to have read him like an open book. That was the beginning of his doom.

He began to visit him more often and became his disciple. His wife Renuka, who thought he was wasting his time, refused to come.

A son was born after three years of marriage. He thought it was by Guru Maharaj's blessings. She thought it had happened naturally. After the birth of his son, influenced by his Guru's teachings, one of them being the control of sex which was essential for the spiritual path, he lost interest in sex. She lost interest in him altogether and fell in love with her colleague, a widower.

By the time his son was eight, Dr Ramakant felt strongly about his son growing up in a spiritual atmosphere and wanted him to attend the Shanti Sadan Boarding School of Guru Maharaj's Ashram which had now shifted to Chhatarpur in Delhi.

Renuka opposed it tooth and nail but he wouldn't relent. Finally, she let him have his way. His son, who was named Arjun by Guru Maharaj, initially refused to go but eventually agreed. Within a year, Renuka asked for a divorce and married her colleague. Guru Maharaj pacified Dr Ramakant by saying that now he could be fully dedicated to his spiritual life. He also told him that a new hospital was coming up and he should take early retirement citing health reasons and take charge of the hospital matters. Along with that, he would also be Guru Maharaj's personal secretary and physician.

But worse things were in store for him. After four years in school his son started hinting that he was being sexually abused by Guru Maharaj. In the beginning Arjun hadn't complained because he thought it was a weird form of blessing. But parents of two other students had withdrawn their children based on similar allegations.

He had a chat with Guru Maharaj who assured him that he was only trying to activate his son's *Muladhara Chakra* that lay in the general area of the reproductive organs. Blinded by devotion he had accepted even that and consoled his son. But the worst was yet to come.

A year later Arjun committed suicide by jumping off the terrace of his fourth-floor dormitory. With the power that Guru Maharaj wielded, political influence was used to hush up the incident. Still influenced by Guru Maharaj, Dr Ramakant refused to file an FIR.

His ex-wife wrote him a bitter letter pointing out what a fool he was and how heartless he had been to their son. Enclosed was a letter from Arjun to his mother written three days before his death begging for her to help him. She tried her best to file a case against Guru Maharaj but couldn't do much. He was too powerful.

At that time, Dr Ramakant thought that everything that had happened was Guru Maharaj's blessings. Even the suicide of his one and only son was, as Guru Maharaj had said, God's way of taking away all attachment. Suspicion would raise its disturbing head off and on but he had managed to sweep it under the rug of surrender.

But now, as he sat alone, looking out of the window, something jolted him out his blind faith. It was Guru

Maharaj's words: 'Jayantilal should be allowed to die. His soul has been pleading with me. After his body dies, his soul will come to my heart.'

When Arjun, his dear Arjun had died, he had said, 'His soul is now free and rests in my heart forever.' How could he have been so blinded by faith. This megalomaniac had fooled him all along for his own selfish needs. Ramakant had lost everything. His beautiful loving wife and his son who had been dearer to him than anything else in this world, all to satisfy this monster.

His body shook uncontrollably as the illusions fell away and he cried as he had never cried in his life. Soon the weeping was replaced by a gust of anger that seemed to rise from the very depth of his being.

He had to stop this drama before any more lives were destroyed. This incarnation of evil had to die. He laughed like a lunatic when he saw how destiny had now placed this monster's life in his hands. No mercy should be shown to such evil-doers. He remembered Krishna's advice to Arjuna: 'Perform your dharma and kill the evil Kauravas.'

'Remain cool,' he said to himself, 'no outward signs of the hatred that is seething inside.'

He washed his face and hands and went to the cabinet where he kept the syringes. He took one out. From the refrigerator he took out the insulin vial and put it in his bag.

It was time for the injection. He walked briskly to Guru Maharaj's luxurious room in the divine abode. The Guru was sitting in an easy-chair waiting for him. Dr Ramakant had to keep his emotions under control. With great effort he put on the expression of utter, wide-eyed surrender that he always had in Guru Maharaj's presence.

This fellow was a clever customer, evil but extremely intelligent. Would he suspect anything? Did he look strangely at him? Perhaps it was just his imagination.

As calmly as possible he opened the bag and took out the syringe. As he was filling the syringe with 100 units of insulin, twice the usual dose, enough to kill him silently, he spoke to Guru Maharaj.

'Maharaj, your blood sugar level has increased. But don't worry, you'll be fine.'

'You know best,' said Guru Maharaj. 'I have always trusted you and you are such a great doctor. Did you talk to Dr Mandira? What did she say about Jayantilal?'

'She said she'll report to you in the morning,' he lied.

Dr Ramakant stuck the needle in Guru Maharaj's thigh, then slowly and steadily injected the insulin.

A great feeling of satisfaction suffused his being. At last, he was doing the good deed, getting rid of an evil man. Sweet revenge for destroying his life and all that he had once loved.

He withdrew the needle and asked, 'Guru Maharaj, have you had your sleeping tablet?'

'No, not yet,' said Guru Maharaj, 'I'll have it now. Can you get it for me from the cabinet there?'

Dr Ramakant got one tablet of Ambien 5 mg and gave it to Guru Maharaj who popped it into his mouth and drank some water. He then stretched himself on his imported luxury bed and said, 'Rama, just switch off the light and close the door as you leave and don't forget to remind Mandira to see me in the morning.'

'As you command, Guru Maharaj,' said the doctor, prostrated, switched off the light and shut the door.

* * *

As he walked away, he smiled to himself. In fifteen minutes the lethal 100 units ml of insulin would take effect. By then, the sleeping tablet would have done its job and the bastard would die in his sleep.

A wave of intense relief spread through his mind. He had done the good deed. He got rid of this evil.

In the morning, he would declare him clinically dead and weep with the rest of the devotees, but no one would know he was actually weeping for his dear son.

The Murder Lisa Helped to Solve

Lisa was the only witness to the murder. Even before it happened she had a strong hunch but could do nothing about it. Sitting in her favourite, green-upholstered La-Z-Boy she watched Mrs Elena Smith sleeping, a peaceful expression on her beautiful face, lips slightly parted, not aware of the grave danger that was approaching.

Elena was a rich heiress who had married a penniless man much below her status, against her parents' wishes. She had supported him constantly until he became a billionaire in his own right, only to discover over the years, that he really did not care for her. He was a philanderer and a crass opportunist and on top of that he had turned into an alcoholic.

For the last three years they had fought almost every night. Alcohol made him violent and thrice he had become quite physical. The last time they had fought he had almost strangled her to death. From where Lisa sat she could see the deep blue marks on Elena's neck.

She had decided to divorce him but he would not agree. For a week now, he had kept quiet, not drinking too much, pleading with her and not being violent. She had nevertheless decided to break free from the beast she had nurtured with care. The lawyers had prepared the papers and she would place them before him and confront him squarely the next morning. Or so she thought.

Lisa was sure something terrible was going to happen. She had been watching Mr Smith closely for many days. He had always loved gardening but for the past week, he had been spending an unusually more amount of time in the garden. At first, she thought he was doing it to avoid contact with his wife. A heated argument would erupt from the most ordinary comment from either side. He had got new saplings to be planted in the garden and was digging pits to plant them, but what intrigued Lisa and caused her to worry was the extraordinary depth of one particular pit he seemed to be digging.

Lisa had a great many sleepless nights trying to figure out why the pit was being dug so deep. Then it suddenly flashed across her mind. He was digging a grave, not in the usual shape but like a circular pit used to plant trees. He would murder his wife and bury the body standing up, fill the pit with earth and fertilizer and plant a tree. Nobody would suspect anything.

Elena had taken a sleeping tablet and fallen asleep. Lisa had a strong feeling that Mr Smith was going to murder Elena when he came back home but could do nothing about it. When Lisa heard the door open, she jumped out of the chair and let herself out of the room through the cat door under the large glass sliding door that faced the balcony near the river. Elena loved to lie on the bed and watch the river flow by. Theirs was perhaps the biggest house by the riverside, in Jupiter, West Palm Beach.

Smith hated Lisa, Elena's grey and white Siamese cat with blue eyes, gifted to her by her mother and resented the loving bond between them. He had kicked her several times when Elena wasn't around, especially when he was drunk. Lisa guessed he would be drunk that night and the first thing he would do would be to kick her.

Lisa placed herself in a strategic position on the outside corner of the glass door, hoping that he would not draw the curtains. It was past midnight. The door opened and Smith staggered in completely drunk. By the light of the bedside lamp, Lisa could see him clearly. One half of the door had been pushed aside to let in fresh air through the mesh door and she could clearly hear Smith screaming.

'Elena!' he shouted. 'Oh, my innocent, darling wife. I bribed that lawyer dude, handsome fellow, and he gave me a copy of the papers. Divorce! Can you hear me? How dare you pretend to sleep when I talk to you? Elena!'

No response. The sleeping tablets had done their work. Elena was sound asleep. He shook her holding her by the shoulders but Elena merely moaned in her sleep, blissfully unaware of the haunting reality. Smith had been working out different plans as to how he could put an end to her life and, in his drunken state, it appeared to him that the perfect opportunity had presented itself right there.

He picked up one of the thick pillows which she always liked to surround herself with. Carefully, he placed it on her face and held it down, tight and firm. After a minute or two she started to struggle as the air supply to her lungs was being cut off. Smith was a strong man so even though she flayed her arms and legs and tried to twist herself away, he held the pillow firmly. In a short while she ceased to struggle. Elena was dead.

Smith took away the pillow and checked her nostrils, no breath. He put his ear to her chest, no heartbeat. He checked her wrist, no pulse. Her body was losing its warmth rapidly. He shook her once more. There was no doubt she was dead. He turned to the glass door, but then who would be there at this time of the night? It was a moonlit night and he could see the river flowing. He had half a mind to carry the dead body and throw it into the river but someone would find her and he would have to provide answers. The best way was to carry the body out and dump it in the pit in standing position as he had planned for many days. Even though the garden was equipped with dim lighting, Smith was not taking any chances and decided to use a flashlight instead.

He slid the door open and noticed something jump up from the grass. He switched on the flashlight and realized it was Lisa, the damned cat he hated so much, her pet she loved dearly. According to Smith, cats were dumb, there was no danger but he would have liked to kill her too. Sometimes Smith imagined he had seen intense hatred in her blue eyes and felt as if she knew how his mind worked. He picked up a stone gargoyle and threw it in her direction but missed. Lisa scampered away.

Smith carried Elena's body in his arms and staggered through the door into the garden. In a few minutes he had reached the deep pit. Carefully he lowered her in standing position. Perfect. Above her head there still was a foot of empty space. He set off to work with his shovel. Half a foot was first filled with mud. Then, he fixed a young long leaf pine, two feet high, in the pit and added more soil until the pit was levelled. He pressed the soil down with his boots and poured some water. The work was done. He looked around to make sure no one was around—not a soul in sight, just some noisy crickets—nothing to worry about. Only, he did not know that Lisa was hiding behind the hedge, watching him.

Back in the house, Smith walked to the bedroom he had been using for the last year ever since his wife had refused to let him sleep with her. He took a swig of his favourite Jack Daniels and lay down. He was tired. The necessary telephone calls could be made in the morning. The last thought that lulled him to sleep was the pleasant memory of sleeping with his sexy secretary Betsy. Elena was completely off his mind his mind.

The next morning at nine, after some coffee and a refreshing shower, he phoned Elena's father, Robert Grey, the rich widower who had once been a Justice of Peace, a prominent citizen of West Palm Beach.

'Hi Bob,' he said. 'Good morning. Is Elena there? When I came home late last night, she wasn't here. I was just checking. You know we have been having a tough time for some time now.'

Robert said she had not and he did not know anything and cut him off abruptly. Robert hated Smith. Then Smith called up the West Palm Beach Police Station and spoke to the police chief, Norah G. Parker. He had met her a few times but he had to be careful. Norah was a good friend of his wife's.

'Hello chief, good morning. This is William Smith. My wife Elena hasn't come back home. I called her father and she hasn't gone there either. This is unusual. Has never happened before. I was tired so I fell asleep, thought she would be back. I woke up twice in the night but noticed she wasn't there. I did not want to disturb you at night so waited until morning. Perhaps you know something, I know you are good friends.'

'Well, Mr Smith, I will talk to detective David Kleine and let you know. He might want to ask you a few questions.'

'Sure, anytime,' Smith said and rang off.

Norah was an experienced officer. She herself had investigated many cases successfully and had mastered the knack of looking beyond the obvious, and in this case she instinctively felt there was something fishy going on.

Elena had been her good friend and on a couple of occasions she had confided in her and spoken about her troubled married life, the violent behaviour of her husband and his excessive drinking habits. Just the other day, she had said that she thought how divorce was the solution but still hoped that he might reform. Norah had suggested that she could perhaps have a chat with Smith. Hoping it might help. Now she regretted being too busy with work and not talking to him sooner. Was it too late now?

Elena's father Robert had called her two minutes ago and said that he suspected something terrible had happened to his daughter. 'Smith is a scoundrel,' was what he said. 'Could have even murdered my daughter.'

Norah telephoned detective Kleine. She had great admiration for Kleine, a middle-aged widower and one of the best detective officers she had seen in her career. Calm, quiet, meticulous and hardworking. Just a month ago he solved a murder case against all odds.

'Morning, chief,' said detective Kleine as he stepped into her office.

'Morning, David. Take a seat. Coffee? No? Okay here is something that would interest you. Could be homicide but can't say anything definite right now.'

She gave him all the information she had. He listened carefully, making notes and when she had finished he said, 'Need to see this Smith guy and talk to him, chief.'

'Sure. There is his telephone number. Good luck.'

'Thanks.'

As soon as he stepped out of Norah's office, David called Smith.

'Good morning, Mr Smith. This is detective David Kleine from the West Palm Beach Police Station. Would like to talk to you. Can I see you at your place in ten minutes?'

'Okay, officer. I will wait for you.'

Lisa, sitting under Elena's bed, heard the conversation. If she had been a tigress, she would have killed him. Small and insignificant as she was, she still planned on nailing him somehow.

Kleine got into his car and drove straight to No. 420 Jupiter, a posh riverside bungalow. As he drove, he was thinking. He agreed with Norah that something was not right. Twenty years in homicide and he knew it when he smelled a rat. Kleine decided that it would be prudent to not raise the topic of his alcoholism or domestic violence with Smith. Surely not now . . .

He parked his car in the driveway and rang the bell. Smith opened the door himself and let him in. 'That was quick, officer. Please come in. Can I get you some coffee?'

'No, that's fine. Please show me your bedroom.'

Smith let him to the bedroom which Elena had been sleeping in for the last one year. Inspector Kleine took a good look at the bed, the sheets and pillows.

'Great view of the river from here,' he said. 'So, this is where you slept last night?'

'Yes, officer,' he lied.

'When did you come home last night?'

'Around midnight.'

'Ah! Quite late. Is that normal?'

'Yes, I usually work late and sometimes have to take clients out for dinner.'

'Did you take someone out for dinner last evening?'

'Yes, one of my clients.' He didn't tell him that he had taken Betsy out for dinner, gotten drunk and had a fight with her.

'Okay, and . . .'

An extraordinarily loud meow ran through the house.

'What's that?' asked the detective, startled.

'Oh! My wife's cat,' said Smith and detective Kleine caught a glimpse of exasperation on his face. He walked out of the door they had come in from and entered a short corridor. There was an open door on the right side. The loud meow came from inside the room. Detective Kleine said, 'If I may,' and entered what was another large bedroom. One of the pillows looked slept on and the sheets on that side were ruffled. On a side table was an empty whiskey glass. The inspector picked it up and smelt it.

From under the bed emerged a grey and white Siamese cat with blue eyes. It brushed against Kleine's trousers and led the way back to the bedroom with a view. The cat jumped on to the bed and Smith shouted angrily, 'Lisa, get down!'

That is when the detective noticed that there was only one pillow in the centre that looked slept on. The cat jumped off the bed, went under and, to the detective's surprise, came out with another pillow. Not able to control his , Smith tried to land a kick but Lisa managed to dodge him and ran out of the room through the cat door.

'Damn,' said Smith, 'that cat makes such a nuisance of itself. Sorry, detective.'

'That's all right,' Kleine said. 'I am okay with cats. I kind of like them.'

Then he picked up the pillow the cat had brought and examined it carefully. There were traces of saliva and vomit on one side and the pillow case was slightly torn as if someone had tugged hard at it. He betrayed no sign of excitement.

'May I take this pillow with me?' he said with a blank expression. 'Might come in handy for the investigation.'

'No problem,' said Smith. The detective noticed he had gone visibly pale.

'So, the glass doors open in to the garden?'

'Yes, my wife loves to look at the trees and the river.'

'Can we open it and step out for a minute?'

'Sure.'

Outside, the detective noticed a pair of gumboots with the soles full of mud. It had rained slightly at night. Someone had walked outside.

'Your boots?' he asked.

'Yes, I do a lot of work in the garden. Fond of gardening.'

Kleine walked into the garden with Smith in tow and looked around. There were many trees, some young, some old, some recently planted—all well looked after. Smith seemed to genuinely be interested in gardening.

As they were about to return to the house, the cat appeared again, meowing and going around a young longleaf pine that looked newly planted. Kleine noticed that there was fresh soil around the tree but said nothing. He pretended that he was not interested. He did not want Smith to know about his growing suspicions. The circular area around the longleaf pine was too small to hide a dead body . . . unless . . . Anyway, nothing had been proved yet. He would investigate carefully. Perhaps there was a grave somewhere on the grounds. 'Strange cat,' was all he said and thought he heard Smith muttering 'God damned cat' under his breath.

As they came back to the house, the cat disappeared again. Detective Kleine said goodbye. 'Might want to ask a few more questions, Mr Smith,' he said. 'Will get back to you.'

'Sure anytime, officer,' said Smith as he saw him off and shut the door. 'Damn cat. Should have got rid of it.'

Detective Kleine walked up to his car, opened the door and put the pillow on the back seat. Out of nowhere the cat leapt into the car, startling him, mewed once and then sat on the pillow. Detective Kleine's cat had died just a week ago. He did not mind having her. He was a widower himself and a cat in the house would make all the difference. Smith seemed to hate the cat anyway. Hadn't he called her Lisa? Kleine shut the door, got into the driver's seat and drove to the police station. 'Lisa, you are safe with me,' he said and Lisa purred as if she understood.

He walked into his office with Lisa and introduced her to his staff. She followed him into his cabin and settled calmly on the rug. Kleine sent the pillow to the forensic lab and noted the important points of the case. Smith certainly seemed guilty of something. Perhaps he was withholding information or did he actually murder his wife? The cat had gone around the freshly planted longleaf pine. Was she pointing out something, although how anyone could bury a dead body in such a small pit puzzled him.

Nothing could be ruled out. He should not be drawing conclusions without concrete evidence. He would wait for the forensic report. He looked at Lisa and an idea took shape in his mind. Worth trying. He got her some cat food and milk during lunch. Lisa lay on the small sofa in his office and fell asleep.

Before anything else, he had to speak to the chief.

Detective Kleine knocked at Chief Norah Parker's door. 'Come on in,' said the chief. 'Sit down. So, what's up?'

Kleine talked and she listened with complete attention. When he had finished briefing her, she said, 'I agree with you, David. Had a chat with Elena's father and he thinks Smith is capable of anything. When the forensic report comes, we'll have more to go by. Knowing you, I am sure you have something up your sleeve. What can I do for you?'

Kleine described his plan. 'What I need is a search warrant signed by judge Pinkerton and also official permission to exhume what I think would be Elena's corpse from under the longleaf pine, although, how one can bury a dead body in such a small pit beats me. Perhaps it's a deep pit and he buried it in a standing position.

If you can get me these documents, I can get to work first thing in the morning, tomorrow.'

The chief said she thought she could manage to get the papers by evening. 'By then the forensic reports would be ready and we can work with more certainty.'

'I will need to take the photographer and a forensic department official to examine the body when it is exhumed. Rowland Brothers' Exhumation Services is a firm I have worked with before. Once the papers are ready I can call them up.'

'Okay, done,' said Chief Norah Parker. 'I am curious to see your feline assistant.'

'She is sleeping in my office. Care to step in?'

'Sure.'

The moment they entered, Lisa woke up and stretched her body as if she was bowing to the chief.

'Good salute,' said Norah laughing. 'Her blue eyes are almost human.'

***

Smith went about his life as if nothing had happened. He sat down to look at his files in his luxuriously appointed office. Betsy was on leave for a few days and he did not like the substitute. He had no interest in women who were not attractive. He leaned back in his swivel chair, thinking about the events from the previous night and the detective's visit this morning. The tiny wound on his wrist where the damned woman had clawed him when she struggled would heal soon. He had a Band-Aid on, which his watchstrap hid quite well. All he needed to do now was control his drinking. But would he have done this had he not been drunk? He wasn't sure. Perhaps he would have, and in a better way maybe. Did the detective suspect something? Would they find anything from the pillow? He was confident he wouldn't be charged; he would hire the best attorney to fight his case if it came to that. In any case, no one would suspect that Elena's dead body was under the longleaf pine he had planted. Pushing the thoughts out of his mind, he picked up the phone and asked for a coffee.

* * *

The forensic report came in at 4 p.m. There were traces of human saliva and vomit, possibly a woman's, along with a bit of human blood that he hadn't noticed. Apart from that they found a few strands of long brown hair.

By 5 p.m. the chief had all the papers ready for him. Kleine called up Rowland Brothers and instructed them to be outside gate 420, Jupiter, by 9 a.m. the next day and wait for him there. He now had the official permit.

After preparing for the next day, Kleine left for his house at 5.30 p.m. and Lisa accompanied him. When they reached his house, Lisa went in without hesitation and wandered about familiarizing herself with the new territory. He sat down on his armchair after an early dinner he had cooked for himself. Lisa sat on the rug and kept looking at him expectantly.

At 10 p.m. he had a shot of Rémy Martin and switched off the lights. Lisa slept on his armchair. The next day, Kleine arrived at the gates of No. 420, Jupiter, and called Smith. Lisa had tagged along. Behind his car was the truck from Rowland Brothers' Exhumation Services and another police car with the photographer and an officer from the forensic department.

'Good morning, Mr Smith, this is detective Kleine here. I am outside your gate and would like to talk to you for a few minutes.'

'So early, detective? Okay, come on in. I am opening the gate.' The remote-controlled gates opened and the detective's car, followed by the truck and the other police car, drove into the drive way. Kleine asked the exhumers to wait in their truck. Lisa decided to stay with them as if she knew what was expected of her. He walked up to the door accompanied by the photographer and even before he could ring the bell, a brown-haired elderly lady opened the door and let him in.

'Mr Smith is in the study, sir.' She led the way.

'Hello, officer. Care to have a cup of coffee?'

'No, thank you. I think I'll get down to business. I have a search warrant and would like to search the grounds. We don't have any suspicions against you,' lied Kleine 'but this is routine.'

'Okay, no problem,' said Smith relieved to hear that the police hadn't established anything against him. So, where would you like to start?'

'In the garden, if I may.'

'Sure.'

Smith led him into the garden from the back door. They walked around until the longleaf pine was in sight. The detective stopped and called Michael, one of the men waiting in the truck.

'Come into the garden on your right side, Michael, and bring Lisa along with your assistants.'

Smith stammered, 'You mean Lisa the cat? I thought she ran away . . .'

'She is safe with me,' said the detective, watching Smith's face carefully.

'Hell,' said Smith. For the first time he felt things weren't going well for him.

The exhumers with their tools, led by Lisa, walked up to the longleaf pine. Lisa went straight to the tree, stopped, turned towards Smith, meowed loudly as if to say, 'I hate you,' and started clawing at the soil.

Just then Elena's father, who looked like a wreck, walked in unexpectedly. 'Called your office, officer, and was told you are headed this way. I had to be here. I am sure this rascal has killed her. I am sure of it! We knew he was bad for our dear girl! How we tried to dissuade her from marrying this brute. She would not listen. It's too late now. My poor girl, look what has happened now!'

'Well, I am not sure about anything, sir,' said detective Kleine. 'It all depends on what we find.'

Smith declined to comment. The thought that he should flee occurred to him but there was no chance. The detective was armed and so was Elena's father.

Kleine said, 'Get to work, guys.'

The exhumers set to work expertly. They pulled the maple tree out. For over a feet and a half there was nothing and then Michael's shovel hit something. He pulled out his shovel, checked it and said, 'Human skin and hair, sir.'

'Okay, now be careful,' said the detective.

Detective Kleine and Lisa moved forward so they could look inside the pit.

'I'll stay here and take care that this guy does not run away,' said Elena's father, Robert, who, along with other inspectors, stood blocking Smith.

In a short while, they had cleared the soil and could clearly see the top of a head. Using their expertise, they managed to unearth and pull out Elena's corpse. That it had rained in the night making the soil loose helped immensely. They laid the body on the grass. Lisa began to mew piteously. It was too much for Elena's father. He burst into tears. The only one who displayed no emotion was Smith. He stood looking at the dead body. Hands folded across his chest. The photographer and the forensic department official went to work.

'Jesus Christ,' exclaimed Michael's assistant.

Detective Kleine called the station and gave instructions to have the body removed to the morgue. Then he took out the handcuffs and walked up to Smith. Smith crumbled.

'All right, all right! Yes!' screamed Smith. 'I confess to killing her,' he said, betraying no emotion whatsoever.

'Mr Smith you are under arrest, charged with the cold-blooded murder of your wife. Whatever you say can and will be used against you in a court of law. You may call an attorney if you please.'

For a moment, detective Kleine thought he saw Lisa smile. 'I think my imagination is running crazy these days,' he muttered to himself.

Mr Robert Grey wanted to take Lisa home but she was reluctant to leave Kleine. It was decided that she would go home with Kleine. They drove away.

The next day the forensic lab confirmed that Smith's blood and the smear on the pillow-case were the same. Smith was charged with first-degree murder and sent to prison without parole.

Detective Kleine fondly named the cat Sergeant Lisa.

Hell Hole

When David Hesler drove his black Audi Q7 that rainy evening from Washington D.C., he didn't have a hint of what was in store for him. He and his wife, Sarah, were proud atheists and rationalists. According to them, the supernatural world of ghosts and haunted houses were figments of imagination of horror-story writers.

Getting to Clarks Town would have taken him an hour or so normally. But the rain was going to delay him. The dark clouds seemed to get denser and denser. In the midst of the furiously blowing wind, the deafening thunder and the flashes of lightning continued unabated.

David looked at his watch. It was about 6.00 a.m. According to the maps on his phone, he would reach his destination at 8.00 a.m.

David loved driving but this drive was turning out to be not so pleasurable. Sarah had told him to postpone it to the next day. She even said she would come along if he went the next day but David feared he might lose the deal if he postponed the trip. It was a good deal. He made plans to check himself into an Airbnb he had located in Clarks Town and decided to meet the agent the next morning.

The farmhouse and the 100 acres of farmland not far from the Airbnb he had booked would, he was confident, be added to the list of his successful real estate deals. The description the agent had provided were excellent and the price was almost throwaway, some kind of a distress sale. All he needed before signing the documents was a proper physical verification of the property so that he could find out why it was being sold at such a low price, plan how to remedy the shortcomings, if any, and sell it off at a much higher price after a couple of years.

That was his specialty. He had made a lot of money this way.

But what excited David more than that was the fact that the Airbnb he had found to stay for the night had been advertised as a two-hundred-year-old house. David loved old houses. Perhaps the owner would be willing to sell it to him. Nice old house not far from D.C. Good for a weekend hangout. Sarah would love it, he thought.

At 7.55 a.m., David reached his destination. *Hell Hole*, No. 600, Bugle Street, Clarks Towns. 'Weird name,' he said to himself.

He liked what he saw. A lovely old, double-storey, brick-walled Victorian house except there was no garden in front. All the houses around were new-style constructions. The thought that it could be a so-called haunted house that no one was willing to buy crossed David's mind, but he quickly pushed the thought away. After all, he had bought, done-up and sold a reportedly haunted house five years ago and his clients continued to send him thanks every year for having sold them a beautiful house. No ghosts. Ghosts were just bullshit!

David drove the car into the open garage on the left of the house, climbed out, took out his overnighter and the paper bag with McDonald's burgers and stepped out on to the white-painted wooden patio.

He opened the electronic lock on the teak-wood front door using the code he had been given, 6896, and was now entering the hall when to his utter surprise, he was greeted by a woman who seemed to have stepped out of history. The clothes she wore and the way she had done up her hair made her seem like she belonged to some ancient period. It was as if she had stepped out of a play, in period costume.

'Welcome to Hell Hole,' she said in a gruff voice. 'I am sure you won't like it here. Don't pretend you don't know me.'

'Thank you,' David said, thinking she must be a housemaid—but why the fancy clothes?—'But no, I don't know you,' he said, confused.

'Yeah! Liar,' she said. 'I need to go and get the girl. I come often but today . . .'

In the dim light of a table lamp which seemed to be the only light that was on, David thought that the left half of her face and arm were deformed, as if severely burnt. Before he could look carefully, she turned and walked through a door on the left.

David switched on the lights. Who was she and why had she walked away abruptly? He went in through the same door, used his flashlight, found the switches and switched on the lights.

It was a rather large medieval kitchen but had all the modern gadgets like a proper electric cooking range and a refrigerator. But there was no one in sight. Perhaps she had gone into the utility room. David quietly opened the door. No one in sight. From the single large, glass-paned window, he could see the backyard. It was still raining, though not so heavily. There was no one there either. He stepped back into the kitchen and shut the door.

And then he heard the sound of a woman chuckling which was instantly replaced by a child's painful wail. For the first time, David felt uncomfortable. 'Ghosts don't exist,' he said to himself. Was fear creeping into his mind? 'This isn't real, David,' he found himself saying, 'someone for some strange reason is playing a prank on you.'

He decided to explore his surroundings. The ground floor consisted of a fairly large study with comfortable leather sofas and a Victorian armchair. On the other side of the passage was a dining room. The kitchen opened into the dining place on one side and the other door on the side through which the mysterious woman had entered and disappeared.

David noticed that the bed sheets, the pillow cases and the quilt were all white, and so were the lamp shades. He brought his overnighter that he had left in the hall and placed it on the reading table. Then he decided to explore the upper floors. He thought he heard the chuckling and the crying coming from upstairs. Perhaps, it was his imagination.

He switched on the stairway lights. Although dimly lit, he could see the staircase and the landing clearly.

He climbed up the imposing staircase. At the first landing was a small door. A note was stuck on the door: 'Do Not Enter the Attic. Keep Out.'

As he continued to climb, David could hear the thumping of his heart. Never in his life had he felt so frightened of the unknown. But he wasn't going to give up, this was a good deal.

There were two bedrooms upstairs and the lights were already switched on.

Comfortable bedrooms with old-fashioned beds and minimum furniture. Both bedrooms had old sepia-toned photographs of a woman and a little girl and a large mirror on the opposite wall. The same pictures in smaller frames were also in the bathroom.

It suddenly struck David that the woman looked like the one he had seen when he entered the house. Was she hiding in the attic? What kind of prank was being played and why?

He decided to sleep in the bedroom downstairs. He felt safer there. As he came out of the bedroom facing the stairs, he took one last look at the picture on the wall and was convinced it was the picture of the same woman except her face wasn't deformed on one side.

He walked down quickly and avoided looking at the attic door. Was it the wind playing tricks on the mind? He thought he heard a woman's voice whispering hoarsely, 'He knows, he knows,' followed by the sobbing of a child.

He went back to the bedroom downstairs, opened his overnighter and changed into his pyjamas. He wanted to have a shower but seeing the picture of the little girl and her mother in the bathroom, decided against it. He had a strange feeling he was being watched.

While returning to the bedroom, he had picked up the brown paper bag with the hamburgers. He now reached for the Glenfiddich Single Malt Whisky from his overnighter. He wore his rubber slippers and came out into the sitting room.

Placing the whisky and food on the table beside the comfortable armchair, he walked to the kitchen, picked up an old-fashioned whisky glass, dropped a few ice-cubes from the refrigerator into the glass and walked back to the sitting room.

In the right-hand corner of the room, there was a large 1960s music box. He turned the knob and soon Beethoven's Symphony Number 5 in C minor filled the room. His favourite. What a coincidence! David had always loved Beethoven's Symphony Number 5.

Easing himself into the armchair, David sipped his whisky and decided to relax. He was kind of tired after driving in the rain. The rain had stopped by then and except for the song, there was total silence, an unnerving one he thought. He finished his first glass in record time and poured himself another. He was feeling good. Two pegs of whisky always made him feel good and relaxed.

There were four more pictures on the walls. The one facing him was a large painted portrait of a man in military uniform. As David looked carefully at it, he realized that face looked startlingly like his own except that the chap in the picture had a walrus moustache. Was he imagining or was the whisky getting to him? He stopped speculating and laughed it off.

The two pictures on either side were photographs, sepia toned, again that of the mother and the child taken separately. On a corner shelf were the toys, mostly pigs and cows. Who were these people? Perhaps the attic held the secrets. Oh yes, he could ask the agent who found him the accommodation. He would know.

His cell phone was dead . . . Quite unusual. The charger would be in his bag but he didn't want to look for it now. 'Will do it when I go to bed,' he said to himself. He had to call Sarah before he slept anyway. As of now, he just wanted to listen to the music and unwind from the tiring journey. It was now Mozart's Symphony Number 40 in G minor. It was as if someone knew his favourites. The song stopped abruptly and from the music box came two voices, the mother's and the child's.

'See, Elizabeth, he has come back after 200 years, your cruel father. He's come back to get rid of us. Let's kill him this time.'

The child's voice said between wails and sobs, 'Yes, Mamma. I don't want be flogged and taken to bed any more. Nooooo . . .'

'Yes, yes. He is a scheming bastard. He can't throw boiling water at me now. Look, he has shaved off his moustache to disguise himself, the scheming devil. Come, let's kill him. He can't fight us now. Let's torture him, my child.'

For the first time, the child's voice laughed gleefully. 'Yes, Mamma. Let's do it.' The female voice chuckled and the music box went off.

David froze with fear. He couldn't understand what was going on but he was scared for his life, which seemed to be in danger. He had never believed in spirits and ghosts but this was real. He had to get out of here.

Summoning all his strength, David jumped out of his armchair and ran to the bedroom. He had left his car keys on the side table by the bed. Entering the bedroom, he grabbed the keys and turned to run. He was still in his pyjamas.

At the door of the bedroom stood the mother and the child. This time he could clearly see that one half of the woman's face was indeed scalded. The little girl's clothes were torn. She was sobbing uncontrollably.

The mother held her close and said, 'Don't worry, Elizabeth, we'll kill him now. Get rid of him forever.' They opened their mouths and David saw sharp and long canines.

He screamed. 'I don't know a thing. Please let me go!' That was when they started laughing. It was a quite an inhuman laughter and sounded like a pack of hyenas. Then they moved towards him.

At that point, the lights went off.

David's only thought was to get out of the damn house as fast as he could. As he ran out of the door, ice-cold clammy arms groped and grappled with him, trying to stop him. A nauseating smell of rotten flesh filled the air.

In a sudden show of strength, David managed to shake them off and ran in the general direction of the hall. 'Catch him!' they screamed. Luckily for him, the door opened when he turned the knob and he was able to get outside. Turning to the right he ran into the garage, unlocked the car and got in. He pulled on the seat belt instinctively and started the car. For the first time in many years, David heard himself saying, 'God! Don't let it stall. Start . . .' The engine came to life, and stepping on the accelerator, David drove out on to the street.

It had started raining again. He tore through the street like a maniac. On the right, he could see the white church and the white walls of the cemetery he had passed on his way to 'Hell Hole'.

As soon as he crossed the cemetery, it came again, the horrible smell of putrid flesh. David looked at the rear-view mirror. They were both in the back seat, the mother and child. With an animal like-snarl, they reached out to strangle him from behind.

David lost control. The car swerved to the right, bounced off the corner of the wall and plunged into the cemetery, crashing through the wooden gate.

The last thing he remembered was that his car steered in the direction of a massive oak tree. With a loud noise, the right side of the car crashed straight into the oak tree and he blanked out.

The next morning the police found a black Audi Q7 which had crashed into a massive tree inside the St Antony's Church Cemetery. At first look, they thought the driver was dead but the air cushion had saved him.

Close to the oak tree were three tombstones: 'Sergeant David Douglas of the Federals. Died 1889. The cruellest man who ever lived. But God is forgiving and merciful. May he rest in peace.'

The second tombstone said: 'Dame Daphne Douglas who suffered so much. God is loving. May she rest in peace.'

The third one said: 'Little Elizabeth Douglas, tortured while still young. May the kind Lord give her peace.'

Close to the graves, from the driver's licence in the glove compartment, they identified the unconscious man and shifted him to the hospital. Both his legs were fractured, the right arm was fractured and he had serious head injuries.

He became conscious in a day or two. But was delirious and kept muttering, 'They are coming for me! They are going to to kill me!'

It took three months of intensive medical and psychiatric care coordinated by his wife Sarah, a qualified psychiatrist, for him to become normal, except that he still feared the dark and slept with the lights on.

But David was now a changed man. He kept the Sabbath, went to the Synagogue and believed in the world of spirits.

Sarah, however, continued to be an atheist.

Sundari Ammu Kutty

Eighty years ago, Tiruvanamkor, the prosperous lush green land of coconut palms, rivers, backwaters and idyllic beaches caressed by the Arabian Sea, was ruled by His Highness Rama Raja Varma.

An epitome of all the qualities that a great ruler should possess as laid down by the ancient scriptures, Rama Raja Varma ruled his kingdom justly and kindly, ever willing to assuage the sorrows of his subjects and at the same time taking stringent action against the wrong-doers.

Not only was he a great strategist, he was also a brave warrior with a formidable army. He defeated the territorial ambitions of the neighbouring kingdown ruler that too, in the first year of coming to power, at barely eighteen. No one dared wage war against his kingdom and peace reigned.

The palace poets and scribes sang highly flattering praises to the king. They described how handsome he was, his golden complexion, how kind and compassionate he was, and so on. The only thing that prevented them from comparing him to the great avatar Rama of Ayodhya, whom the poet Valmiki described as the *Maryada Purusha*, ideal man or a righteous king, was that unlike that Rama, this Rama Raja Varma was a bachelor. At the age of thirty-eight he was still unmarried except in the eyes and doting heart of Sundari Ammu Kutty.

The royalty of Tiruvanamkor believed and practised the matriarchal system, which meant that the son of the king did not succeed the throne; his sister's son or his nephew did. Was that the reason why he remained unmarried? To keep his life less complicated? Or as some loyal subjects said, was it because he was very spiritual and wanted to maintain celibacy? No one knows for sure but for Sundari Ammu Kutty, he was her consort who had married her when he was thirty-eight and she, a mere sixteen years old. Or so she thought.

Sundari Ammu Kutty was a descendant of a Nair *tharavaad* (family). In their blood ran the 'dance of the enchantress', Mohiniattam. Her grandmother and great-grandmother had been celebrated Mohiniattam dancers, descendants of devadasis who danced before the gods. Her grandmother Amini Kutty Amma had been a dancer in the then Maharaja's court.

Her mother Devaki Amma was on her way to becoming a great dancer but had to abandon Mohiniattam. The Maharaja who then ruled Tiruvanamkor had banned Mohiniattam as being a degenerate dance form.

Several years after the ban, poet Vallathol Narayana Menon started a Kalamandalam, a university for the revival of traditional dances, Kathakali, Koodiyattam and Mohiniattam.

Vallathol decided to clean up Mohiniattam of all the crude sexual overtones it had gathered and bring it out in its pristine purity of refined amorous expressions, subtle nuances of love and romance. Mohini, the enchantress's fluid movements, gestures and coy glances were an imitation of the spiritual love of the *gopi*s for their Lord Krishna and the pain of separation concluding with the ultimate ecstasy of union.

Ammu Kutty had from childhood evinced an interest in dancing and at the age of thirteen was allowed to join Kalamandalam by her mother.

Trained by legends like Orikkaledath Kalyani Amma and Chinnammu Amma, Ammu Kutty excelled in nritta and nritya, displaying the *Lasya* form of graceful, gentle and expressive conveying of emotions as well as pure dance movements which laid stress on the rhythmic aspects. At the age of fifteen she gave her solo performance at the Mahavishnu temple.

The divan of Tiruvanamkor witnessed her performance and gave her the title of *Sundari*, 'beautiful', and henceforth she became Sundari Ammu Kutty. This led to her being invited to perform at the palace for the Maharaja. She was sixteen when she entered the Travancore Palace to dance before His Highness Sri Rama Raja Varma.

It was a private gathering in the durbar hall, with only the royal family, the divan and a few officials including Col Tod, the British resident.

Dressed in the white silk and gold-embroidered traditional Mohiniattam costume and wearing beautiful golden anklets, bangles, finger and toe rings, a diamond-studded nose ring and large gold *jhumka*s in both her ears, that swung gently when she shook her head, Ammu Kutty looked gorgeous. It was as if Menaka, the *apsara* damsel who danced in Indra's court, had decided to dance before the earthly king.

She was naturally fair complexioned and with a rose blush on her cheeks and bright red lipstick she looked stunning.

Ammu had only seen the Maharaja's picture in a ceremonial dress two years ago and had instantly fallen in love. Now as she saw him face to face, dressed in a simple white, *Kashav*-bordered dhoti and white silk shirt, with a touch of sindoor on his handsome brow, she was overwhelmed.

As she danced the *Ashtapadi* to the music of her expert accompanist, and expressed the various moods of *Vipralambha*, separation, her soul was transformed into Radha and in the Maharaja she saw her beloved Krishna, teasing her, keeping her away, embracing her and so on. Her beautiful big eyes, made even more beautiful by the black kajal, flirted amorously with the eyes of the Maharaja, who to all external appearances sat firm and composed. But was he really? What was the state of his heart as this goddess danced before him so charmingly?

Though he appeared outwardly calm, deep in his heart the bachelor king was experiencing all the emotions she depicted. Once or twice his eyes met hers and he thought he was going to lose control. The intoxicating jasmine fragrance that emanated from the flowers in her hair transported him to Vrindavan. He was Krishna and she Radha, and they were making love. For the first time, Rama Raja Varma understood the language of love and its manifold mysteries.

Her second and last number was Maharaja Swathi Tirunal's composition '*Poonthen nermozhi sakhi . . .*'

The Maharaja was so absorbed in the imagery of the bee sucking the nectar of love that when the dance was over he still remained with his eyes closed as if in a trance. It was only when his sister whispered to him, 'Tampurane, the performance is over,' that he opened his eyes and saw Sundari Ammu Kutty standing still before him. And then she swayed and was going to fall when in an unprecedented and unexpected move, the Maharaja leapt and caught her in his arms.

She was muttering, 'Krishna, *ente* Krishna,' her eyes locked into his. He wanted to say my Radha and raise her lips to his, but with great effort he controlled himself, not wanting to go against the decorum of the court. 'Can someone take care of her,' was all he said, and handing her over to female palace attendants, went back to his throne.

With a strange smile on his face, Col Tod said, 'Great performance, Your Highness, and the girl's a stunner. Wonder if she would be willing to dance at the British Residency.'

Rama Raja Varma felt his anger rise. If he had been the king a hundred years ago Col Tod would have lost his head. Under the circumstances, the Maharaja controlled his anger, smiled and reluctantly said, 'You need to ask her mother. I think, Colonel. I have no idea.'

The palace maids took her into the inner chamber and in a short while she opened her eyes and appeared normal. She and her mother were then led to the durbar hall.

The Maharaja gifted her with many gold coins and instructed the divan to issue her a certificate declaring her a jewel among dancers, *'Nritya Ratnam'*. He told her mother,

'You have such a talented daughter and so beautiful! We are pleased. Perhaps we shall see her again.'

Her mother bowed low and said, 'We are so honoured, Your Highness. Your word is our command. We should be leaving now if you give us permission.'

'All right,' said His Highness. 'Look after your daughter well.'

As they turned to leave, Ammu said loudly to her mother, 'But Mother, I don't want to go back. I love him. He is my spouse, my Krish—.' Before she could complete her sentence, her mother shut her mouth with her hand and whispered, 'Come, let's go.'

She kept protesting as she was taken away by her mother.

In the durbar hall there was a stunned silence. Nobody spoke. The divan looked at the king, while Col Tod excused himself and went away. The king sat silently staring at the doorway. His sister spoke to him, 'Tampurane, let's go for dinner. Then you must get some sleep. We believe you are tired.'

The Maharaja got up and walked towards his private chamber. 'I am not hungry,' he said, lost in thought.

* * *

For a long time he couldn't sleep, which was quite unusual. Scenes from Ammu Kutty's Mohiniattam kept replaying in his mind. The amorous flirting eyes, the gentle fluid motion of her body, the red sensuous lips, the fragrance of jasmine as he had held her close to him . . .

How wonderful it would be if she could be his forever, sleeping beside him, embracing him, whispering words of love. With supreme effort he pulled himself together. No, he wouldn't make her suffer. Following the custom of matriarchal succession, Ammu's and his offspring would never inherit the throne. His nephew, his sister's son, would become king after his death. He was much older than her and would probably die before her and he knew she would be ill-treated. It had happened before in the royal family. No, he would not succumb to temptation and make her life hell. She may suffer the pangs of separation for a while for he knew she had fallen in love with him, as he too had. Somewhere in his mind he thought that by not making her his own he was doing better than the great Lord Rama who had to send his beloved Sita away to prove to his subjects that he followed the model code of conduct.

Past midnight he fell asleep and dreamt that he had married Sundari Ammu Kutty and that they were sleeping together in the royal chambers.

* * *

As for Ammu, from that fateful day, she lived an imaginary life. Her mental balance disturbed, she fancied herself married to the Maharaja. She insisted on being called *Tamburati*.

Her mother was a wealthy widow and they lived in a large *taravad* bungalow in Perinthani not far from the ancient temple of Mahavishnu. She had never been the legal wife of her husband, a royal from the Quilon branch of the family. She was his concubine. Before his death he had gifted them the big house they lived in and a large tract of paddy and coconut plantation in the outskirts of the city so that Ammu, his dear daughter, would not suffer penury. He was a cruel man and after the first few years of their relationship, they made no secret of hating each other, but he loved little Ammu.

Having lived through the pain and shame of living as a concubine, Ammu's mother Devaki Amma was clear and determined about one thing. Either the Maharaja married her daughter legally which was a remote possibility or she would keep Ammu away from him.

She had met the divan who had known Ammu's father and requested him for an appointment with the Maharaja. She was refused. She tried again for an audience and explained what her daughter was going through. Meanwhile, she dealt with her precious daughter who seemed to have gone mad.

Ammu Kutty had a picture of the Maharaja in his royal robes, complete with the pearl-decorated crown on a small ivory-inlaid, rosewood table in one corner of her room. She had removed the pictures of all other deities. Her only God was the Maharaja—to whose picture she offered incense, performed her puja, offering flowers and sandalwood paste, and waving the brass lamp.

She slept embracing her deity and holding him close to her body. She woke him up in the morning and wiped him clean with a wet towel. Then she placed him back on the table, saying, 'O! My Krishna, my God, don't leave your Radha ever. Wait, I'll get you breakfast.'

When the maid brought breakfast, she would offer some to him, coax him to eat and only then ate the rest. She would then adorn herself in the Mohiniattam costume and dance before him for hours. When lunch came the same procedure was followed; after which she put the picture beside herself in her bed and took an afternoon siesta.

In the evening he was put back on his pedestal and offered tea and *vadas*. With tears in her eyes she would again sing the song describing the pangs of separation till dinner time. Then she would imagine eating dinner together and climbing into the bed with her.

At midnight, her mother and the maids would try to pacify her when she would wake up suddenly, realize that she was merely holding a picture, and weep piteously, 'Come my love, I can't live without you.'

Twice she had attempted to run away saying, 'I am going to the palace,' but was caught and brought back.

* * *

Her poor mother tried everything she could. First Dr Pillai, a well-known psychiatrist from the Uloorpara mental hospital. was consulted. He prescribed various medications which she refused to take. He thought shock therapy might help but her mother was not willing to put her daughter though the terrible treatment. She had seen one of her uncles undergo the painful treatment. He never became normal.

Then came an assortment of astrologers, vaidyas and exorcists who claimed that she was possessed by the soul of an ancient Maharani. Their remedies didn't work. Ammu Kutty was still blindly in love and love needs no explanation. She was, in her mind, married to the Maharaja. She ate with him, slept with him, worshipped him and danced for him. Even her dreams were solely about him.

Her mother tried once more to petition the palace with regard to her daughter's condition and her desire to meet the Maharaja, but there was no response. Her dignity hurt, she stopped trying and decided to look after her daughter, under all circumstances.

Adoration and admiration for the king was replaced by hatred. As far as she was concerned, it was he who was responsible for her daughter's state. Every evening she broke two coconuts in the Ganapathi temple outside the fort. One for her daughter to get well and another for the king, praying he suffers the karmic effect of reducing her daughter to such a state.

* * *

Meanwhile, people in the palace noticed that His Highness Rama Raja Varma was a changed man. No playing golf with the British resident, no tennis, no horse-riding. He had turned into an introvert and avoided public functions as much as possible. He began to pen love-soaked, romantic poetry in Malayalam.

He just had one meal a day and would daydream for hours at length. Tongues wagged in court. The whispered rumours ranged from, 'The Maharaja is suffering from depression, he is in love with Sundari Ammu Kutty,' to 'Someone saw him slipping out at the dead of night to meet her, perhaps he is possessed.' But no one dared to say anything openly.

The one habit he didn't discard and which he held sacred was his daily visit to the Mahavishnu temple. Wearing a dhoti, the upper part of his body bare, he would drive in the antique palace car to the temple at dawn where he would have the darshan of Mahavishnu, bow down with great humility, take the sacred prasad made of milk, honey and banana, apply the sanctified sandalwood paste on his forehead and return to the palace.

* * *

Ammu Kutty came to know of the Maharaja's regular trips to the temple. One day, early in the morning, much before dawn when the maid was fast asleep, Ammu Kutty jumped out of the large French window of her bedroom, climbed over the rear gate which was usually unguarded and walked briskly along the narrow streets that led to the temple of Mahavishnu. It took her around ten minutes.

The temple door usually opened at 4:30 a.m. for *Nirmaalyam*, the first worship of the deity.

She entered the temple, had a quick view of the deity who was being made ready for the morning worship and hid herself in the temple premises behind the massive granite pillars, for she knew that when the Maharaja with his Nair bodyguards came for darshan, all other visitors except the priest were kept out of the temple. In her hand was a fragrant jasmine garland she had acquired the previous night and kept fresh, covering it with a wet cloth. She was waiting for her love, her lord, her consort.

The Maharaja arrived and entered the sanctum sanctorum with a small number of sword-wielding Nair soldiers. He had the darshan of the just decorated deity, offered his obeisance, bowed down, and allowed the priest to mark his forehead with sweet-smelling sandalwood paste. Then he accepted the flower garland which was on Mahavishnu's neck in his hand, tasted a pinch of the prasad and was turning to go, when the unexpected happened. From behind one of the massive pillars, darted a young and beautiful woman with a garland in her hand. Nimbly scaling the three steps to the sanctum sanctorum, she hung the jasmine garland on the Maharaja's neck, saying, '*Tamburane*, you are mine forever.'

The guards recovered from their momentary surprise and whipped out their swords. The Maharaja shouted, 'Wait!' but Ammu, seeing the gleaming swords, stepped back, lost her balance on the steps that lead to the sanctum and fell down, her head hitting one of the massive pillars. '*Bhagwan*e, O Lord,' was the last word she uttered.

'Put away the swords!' the Maharaja screamed, seething with anger which was replaced instantly by intense, heart-wrenching grief.

With the garland still on his neck, he walked to Ammu's immobile body, sat down and took her in his lap. Her eyes were closed and her body was cold. 'Ammu Kutty . . .' he whispered. No answer. She was dead, a massive wound where her head hit the pillar.

H.H. Rama Raja Varma stood up and said, 'Inform her mother and summon the palace doctor immediately.' Then he turned and walked out of temple, got into the car and returned to the palace. Her mother arrived and wept inconsolably. The doctor declared Sundari Ammu Kutty dead due to a head injury. What he didn't know was that the soul of Ammu Kutty was waiting for the Maharaja to join her in *Vaikuntum,* the abode of Lord Mahavishnu, where she had been accepted instantaneously.

* * *

In the palace, the Maharaja's health took a turn for the worse. He had no appetite and stopped eating. Doctors and traditional vaidyas were consulted and medicines prescribed but to no avail. He became thin and emaciated.

The attendant who took turns to look after him reported that every night the Maharaja talked in his sleep, saying, 'Ammu, I am coming,' and sometimes even wept.

One night as the full moon shed its cool light through the glass panes of the Maharaja's bedroom window, he woke up and according to the nurses who were with him looked at the moon with wide open eyes, and said, 'Sundari, I am coming. I can see you. Stretch out your hand, let me hold it. Ammu . . .' Then he held both his hands to his heart, cried in pain, 'Ahh! Ahh!' and became motionless. The doctor who was summoned declared him dead due to a 'massive heart failure'.

After death, Rama Raja Varma and Sundari Ammu Kutty now lived together as husband and wife in *Vaikuntam,* loving each other and serving Lord Vishnu to their hearts' content.

On earth, the love of the Maharaja and the dancer Sundari Ammu Kutty, the immortal lovers, became the subject of many love songs sung by the bards and written by the poets. The name Sundari Ammu Kutty became synonymous with the definition of a true lover.

The Thief

The temptation was irresistible. The recently renovated colonial bungalow was situated on a deserted beach on the Mahabalipuram Road, thirty kilometres from Chennai, and hardly 100 metres from the sea.

In the surrounding darkness of a moonless night, illuminated at intervals by mild streaks of lightning and a malfunctioning, fluorescent street-light, the tall building with its small, dimly lit upper-floor window, stood in total isolation.

The rain started to lash down heavily.

Sambandam, alias Sambu, an orphan aged twenty-five, handsome high-school dropout and out of jail only a month ago after serving his third term for burglary and assault, walked quickly towards the big iron gate. He was filled with a peculiar obsession to break in—a feeling he had learnt to recognize—dangerous yet exciting.

It was just midnight. Both sides of the road were empty. The only sound was that of the sea. The jeans and T-shirt he was dressed in, and the rucksack on his back were all drenched in the rain. Soaked to the skin, he hesitated for a second before pushing open the gate and stepping in.

81

He had been watching the house for the last ten days and knew that there was neither a dog nor a watchman on the ground. He was also sure that there was no one in the house.

It seemed to be a kind of spiritual retreat. Half a dozen or so people, some of them foreigners, visited the house every day and meditated on the beach. But no one except the young Indian couple stayed during the night. That evening even they had driven off in the white Gypsy, which otherwise was always parked on the grounds.

He discreetly kept an eye on the house from seven in the evening, making sure they weren't around and it was safe to go in. They hadn't come back and he hoped they wouldn't return either, not at this late an hour. If they did, well, he knew how to get away.

A six-foot-high compound wall encircled the sandy, two-acre ground on which the bungalow stood. He briskly walked down the brick-lined driveway into the shelter of the portico. It continued to rain.

Having viewed the house from all angles for many days, Sambu had meticulously worked out how he was going to get in, that is, when the opportunity came—as soundlessly as possible.

In his trade Sambu was an acknowledged expert. He removed the black rucksack from his back, took out the pen torch which he had wrapped up in a waterproof polythene bag, directed the beam on the front door and tried the knob slowly.

As expected it was secured by a Godrej night latch which was fixed on the inside but could also be locked from the outside. He had all the necessary locksmith's tools but his plan was different.

Aided by the torch he walked to the rear of the house and checked the back door. No lock on the outside, again as expected. It was probably bolted from inside with tower bolts.

He went round to the right side of the building, stopped and looked up at the ventilator of one of the two ground-floor bathrooms. It was just a few inches above his head. Seemed accessible.

He smiled to himself, for once more he had been proved right. Most people thought that doors and windows must be strong and secure. But few gave much thought to the lowly ventilator. Ventilators, in his experience, were the best entrances for burglars and the easiest to dismantle.

With it still raining heavily with occasional thunder, he took out a large screwdriver and proceeded to remove the screws from the iron grill which was fixed to the three-foot-by-two-foot wooden frame. First he unscrewed the top half—standard procedure. It was still raining heavily with occasional thunder.

Carefully, he detached the grill and placed it down on the grass. Next, he pulled out the five slanting glass strips from their grooves, making as little noise as possible, and placed them outside the grill.

Then, holding the lower part of the ventilator frame with his hands he lifted his lean and agile, five-foot-ten-inch body up until he could look into the bathroom. It was dark inside.

With little effort he brought half his body into the bathroom, the rest dangling outside. Slowly, using his hands and hips, he wriggled in and dropped down on the tiled bathroom floor, breaking the fall with his outstretched arms.

Switching on the torch he took out the small crowbar he always carried from the rucksack and stuck it in his belt. It was a versatile tool; useful for breaking open locks, prying open cupboards, even safes, and excellent for self-defence. He had once defended himself successfully from being strangled to death by an ex-wrestler and had narrowly missed being hauled in for murder. The feel of the cold hard iron steadied his nerves.

All was quiet. He turned the knob of the bathroom door, opened it and entered into what appeared to be a large hall. He didn't want to risk switching on the lights at the moment.

With the help of his flashlight he made a quick survey. On one side of the hall were two bedrooms and on the other a spacious dining hall and kitchen. At the far end of the hall, beside the staircase, was the back door. It had no lock and was shut with tower bolts.

He pulled the bolts open, opened the door just to make sure he could make a quick getaway in case of an emergency and bolted it shut again.

He took note of the CTV, the sound systems and expensive-looking clock in one of the bedrooms. The hall seemed bare except for a huge Persian rug and a divan near the entrance. Above the divan was a life-size portrait of a Jesus-like figure.

Nimbly, he climbed up the granite staircase and reached the landing. He decided he would first take a good look at the room where the light was on. People left the lights on in their houses to give the impression that they were inhabited, a ruse which couldn't fool even the most ordinary burglar.

The upper floor seemed to consist of only one bedroom and a smaller hall. The bedroom door was open. From the landing he could see the small dim reading lamp placed on the ledge of the narrow window, under which was a writing desk and chair. On one side was a small door probably leading to the bathroom and beside the bathroom door was a medium-sized steel safe.

In the middle of the room was a mosquito-curtained double-bed with white linen. The lovely white telephone on the little table beside the bed attracted him, a fancy piece worth carrying away.

He shifted his attention again to the bed, peered inside the mosquito net, took a closer look inside . . . and froze.

No . . . it couldn't be. What he had, at first sight, thought was a heap of white sheets was actually a human body; petite with only a pale little face framed by silver-white tresses, uncovered.

It was a frail old woman, probably dead.

For the first time since entering the room, Sambu smelled a dead animal.

'Bolt!' said the little voice in his head. Sambu moved to obey, when the lights suddenly went off. A nameless and intense fear now gripped his soul. Forgetting even his torch, Sambu lurched in the direction of the door.

Disoriented by the sudden darkness, he stumbled and hit the bedroom door. It shut with a loud bang. His torch went flying from his hand. The crowbar slipped from under his belt, fell with a clang and rolled away.

In the silence that followed, Sambu found himself leaning against the bedroom door. The faint odour seemed to have increased. He was fumbling to locate the door-handle when the lights came on as suddenly as they had gone.

The mosquito curtains were parted. On the bed, her feet hanging down, sat a petite elderly lady in a flowing white nightdress, her long hair a silvery grey. Her dark serene eyes were fixed on him. There was no sign of panic or agitation.

Sambu shivered. His hair stood on end. Was she a ghost? Where was that dreadful odour coming from? If she was not an apparition, what was she doing all alone in this house?

Her calm and clear voice broke the silence.

'Tell me,' she said speaking in Tamil, 'who on earth are you and why are you in my bedroom at this hour making an awful racket? Now, don't stand there gawking like an idiot. Pull that stool, sit down and explain.'

Sambu had no option other than to sit in the cane armchair chair that stood against the wall.

All sorts of questions were racing in his mind. Who was this little old lady? He had never seen a face so tranquil and kind, and yet so august. How could she sleep all alone in this isolated house? Had she no fear? 'At least,' he said to himself, 'she isn't a ghost.'

Looking at her sitting on the bed all alone, a strange, almost pleasant, feeling began to take hold of his heart. He could not define it.

'What's your name?' she asked.

'Sambandam. They also call me Sambu,' he said and a second later wondered if he should have given her a false name.

'*They* means *who*?'

'My . . . sisters.' Again the truth. What was happening to him? 'I have three.'

'And what are their names?'

'Sindu, Bindu and Shamala.'

'Look,' she said. 'Keep telling me the truth as you are doing now and maybe I can help you become a better man. Don't you want to earn some honest money, have a home, look after your sisters . . . father and mother . . .?'

'I don't have a father or a mother. They died long ago.'

'Oh! I am so sorry. Anyway, it breaks my heart to see that a young and promising man like you has turned into a criminal. I bet you were about to burgle my house. Aren't you ashamed of stealing and slinking about like a nocturnal animal? Doesn't matter, you tell me the whole truth about yourself and I promise I will find some good work for you. Forget what you were and face the world bravely. Let tomorrow be a new day.'

For the first time a stranger was being so kind to him. A lump formed in his throat. With great effort he managed to stop himself from crying and started talking.

'Amma,' he said, 'I am going to tell you everything, but please put that gun away. I swear by my mother and Muniaandi, our tutelary deity, that I will not cause you harm. You are the first person who has been so kind to me, that too after knowing I am a criminal.'

'Don't worry about the gun,' she said, putting it away. 'It's my grandson's toy gun anyway,' she laughed. 'Okay, now tell me.'

So Sambandam told her everything. How his father had died in a scooter accident when he was barely ten and how his mother, who meant the world to him, had a heart failure and passed away when he was thirteen years old. He told her how he and his younger sisters, then aged six, eight and ten, had struggled to keep themselves alive.

He had been a bright student, but there was no one to guide or support him. He had dropped out of school and has started out as a pickpocket. And now he was a full-fledged burglar. He also told her how he had almost become a murderer when he had in desperation hit the watchman of one of the houses he had attempted to burgle—with a crowbar. Luckily, the man, a retired wrestler, had survived.

'Amma, after serving my last sentence, when I walked out of the jail some months ago, I resolved to change my ways, but Amma, who would help a criminal? Couldn't find a job even as a waiter. Most people in this locality know my past.

'I have to look after my sisters. I love them. They are the only ones I have left in this world. Often I think of going away somewhere where no one knows me but what about my sisters?'

'Come here,' she said.

Sambu walked up to the bed.

'Sit here beside me.'

'No, Amma. I will sit down on the floor.'

She softly stroked his head and face.

Tears rolled down Sambu's cheeks. 'Amma . . .' was all that he could bring himself to say.

After a while, she said lovingly, 'All right, Sambu—may I call you Sambu? The past has now been wiped out by your tears. So let's think of the future. Would you like to work for me? I need a young and healthy man. All you need to do is be my companion. I will pay you well.'

'Anything you say, Amma.'

'Okay, so now, a new chapter begins.'

'Thank you, Amma.'

For the first time in so many years he felt cleansed, unburdened and as free and light as a butterfly. Yet something bothered him. Was it the fact that the lady had hardly said anything about herself? It was strange that he had begun to trust a total stranger. But then she seemed so intimate, so open and defenceless, like his long-lost mother. No, it was something else. Then what? Oh yes! He now remembered, the sickly odour of decaying flesh. It was still there. Sometimes weak, sometimes strong. He decided to ask her frankly.

'Amma, I smell peculiar, rotten odour and . . .'

'Yes, yes, I know. I think there is a dead rat somewhere. You must help me find it and clean up the place.'

The shrill ring startled him. Someone was pressing the doorbell. By the alarm clock on the table beside the bed, it was 3.00 a.m.

Fear once again had him on his feet. Who could be ringing the doorbell at this hour? Was this all a plot?

'Sambu, don't worry,' she said. 'I'll take care of everything. If anybody asks, say you are my nurse. Come, give me a hand. Let's go downstairs.'

Sambu helped her stand up. She held his hand and they walked down the staircase with a little difficulty. 'Sprained my ankle,' she said. 'Takes longer to heal, you know, when you are old. I wonder who is at the door.'

When they had reached the front door, she switched on the lights and said loudly, 'Who is it?'

'Police Constable David, madam. On my regular beat,' said a gruff voice. 'Saw one of your bathroom ventilators open and heard noises. I thought I will investigate. Sorry to wake you up, madam, but is everything all right?'

'All fine, Constable David. Thanks. Actually, the carpenters were working here today. They must have forgotten to shut it. Wait, I'll open the door.'

Sambu's heart sank. David knew him by sight. Before he could stop her she had unlocked the door and the policeman stepped in. It had stopped raining and the sound of the waves came clearly.

Sambu and the policemen stood staring at each other. The policeman's mouth fell open. He seemed to be at a loss of words for a moment. Then he said, 'Madam, this man . . .'

'I know, I know,' said the lady. 'Sambu has reformed and I have employed him as my personal attendant.'

'Well, madam, do what you think is right, but don't tell me I didn't warn you.'

'That's alright. Thank you. Care to have a cup of tea?'

'No thank you, madam. I'll be on my way. You there, Sambandam, watch out. Any complaints from madam and I'll do—you know what.'

'Yes, sir, Vanakam sir.'

Sambu helped her shut and lock the door after the policeman's departure. She said she couldn't sleep after 3.00 a.m. So he followed her instructions and brewed some excellent tea. As they sat sipping the tea in the drawing room she told him about herself.

'I am a widow,' she said, 'and have no children born of my body but I believe that the human race is one extended family. From now on you are one of us, you are family. One of my children. My name is Anitha but to you I am Amma.'

She pointed to the portrait of the Jesus-like figure he had seen back when he had entered the room. 'That's my guru. We simply call him Appa, father. Now help me go upstairs. It's time to begin my meditation. Perhaps one day you would like to learn how to meditate.

'If you are hungry, eat some bananas. They are on top of the fridge, and sleep here on the sofa. Tomorrow, I will make all pukka arrangements for you and also talk to you about the benefits of prayer and meditation.'

'What about the dead rat, Amma? I'll look for it and throw it out.'

'Oh! Don't worry. Doesn't bother me much. Anyway, it's much less now, it has stopped pouring. So just open all the windows and light a few incense sticks. You will find them in a wooden box besides the phone upstairs. Tomorrow morning you can clean up.'

He led her upstairs and after she had sat on the bed, he opened the windows to let in fresh air and lit the agarbattis. Then, on an impulse, he kissed her feet and said good night.

'No need to do that,' she said affectionately as Sambu shut the door and left.

Sambu went downstairs. It took him ten minutes to fix the ventilator which he had dismantled. Then he washed his hands and feet and stretched himself on the sofa. Instantly he fell asleep.

That night he was finally free of the terrible nightmares that habitually jolted him wide awake in the middle of the night, sweating and trembling. Instead, he dreamt of beautiful hills and dales, lovely, sweet-smelling flowers of all kinds, bathed in the glory of the golden sun that was rising in the horizon.

For him, it was the beginning of a new day—a new life.

The Dimwitted Genius

Kitcchu's coming into the world was indeed unique. Not that his mother had any visions of God or heard celestial music like they say in the biographies of saints and avatars. Nothing of that kind. The music that blared from a loudspeaker somewhere, not far from the paddy fields his mother was working in, was a communist propaganda song 'Saha kalae; munnnotu . . .' that exhorted the comrades to move forward.

Lalitha, his mother, was an extraordinary woman in her own right. Born in a rich, cultured and orthodox Namboodiri Brahmin family, she had long ago broken free from the shackles of caste and creed and daringly married Chandu Nair, an agriculturist and landlord. From Lalitha Antarjanum, she became Lalitha Nair and was of course excommunicated from her clan. Not that she cared. It was not an easy step to take in the Kerala of the 1920s but she was a brave woman. Life became even more difficult after her husband died one year after her son, Kitcchu, was born.

Coming back to Kitchhu's birth, he was born in a paddy field. His mother had shocked and scandalized everyone by deciding to work in the paddy fields, breaking all societal norms, alongside the women labourers who sowed and harvested the rice. She was pregnant with Kitcchu, full nine months, and the local vaidya had predicted delivery any day and advised her rest, but Lalitha insisted that she would be fine.

That day the harvesting was in full swing. Lalitha was reaping ripe crop of *Zeeraga Chemba* rice with her sickle when the pain started. About fifty ladies were working on the field. On one side of Lalitha, stood Chellamma and on the other, Karupayi.

On the bund not far from there stood a big jackfruit tree. Lalitha said to Chellamma, 'Chellamma, help me get to the shade of the jackfruit tree and run up and get the village midwife. It has started to hurt.'

With Chellamma's help she reached the jackfruit tree. The pain was acute now. She felt like clinging on to something steady. She clutched the stout lower branch of the jackfruit tree and moaned in pain. But it was all over in less than a minute.

Effortlessly the baby came out and fell, his head hitting the red earth under the jackfruit tree, with a thud.

Exhausted, she lay under the shade and heard the first cry of the baby boy.

The village midwife arrived and took charge of the mother and child. No external injury except a slight reddish bump on the crown of his head. They were shifted home in a bullock cart because Chandu Nair had gone to the town in his little Fiat Premier.

* * *

One hundred light years away, in planet Swarga that revolved around the star Bhargo, a high-level meeting was in progress, called by its highly evolved and advanced beings.

Shringa, the ruler, spoke to his seven ministers, the rishis as they were known. 'There is hope for the Earth,' he said. 'The two observers we had—as you know very well—sent down to *Bhuloka*, planet Earth, have reported that they found one ideal humanoid who could be the Earth's saviour. He was born yesterday, Earth time, while his mother was in standing position.

'Our observers say that his head hit the earth as he fell out of the womb, as planned and executed by the three scientists we had sent down as soon as the mother became pregnant.

'The impact of the fall has incapacitated that part of the infant's frontal lobe which keeps the brain of humanoids conditioned to only three dimensional experience and thinking.

'As you know, this was done deliberately by our ancestors through genetic modification because it was all that was necessary for their progress at that time, with the provision that this limitation could be deactivated by a strong physical impact on the upper part of the frontal lobe under special circumstances.'

One of the elders said, 'Yes, we know that and now that the limitations are removed, I think attempts must be made to speed up his access to the fourth dimensions and secrets of sound.

'There isn't much time. Planet Earth's destruction that is fast approaching must be stopped somehow. The built-up anger and violence must be dissolved. Compassion must be generated before someone presses the nuclear button. The negative forces must be kept at bay and the secret of acoustics and musical chanting must be revived. Bhuloka was given the Sama Veda by our ancestors but no one knows its secrets any more there.

'I trust, the observers have been briefed sufficiently to implement our plans.'

Shringa spoke, 'Yes, the boy will be kept under observation and sufficient inputs will be given at the appropriate time.'

The meeting concluded with everyone sitting in a circle and meditating with closed eyes for a short time before they dispersed. Soft music of a low frequency played in the background.

The observers were keeping a constant watch but discreetly, so that the humans, humanoids as they called them, suspected nothing. There were prepared to intervene when and where necessary.

* * *

Kitcchu's father died exactly one year after his birth—a major cardiac failure. Lalitha single-handedly brought up the baby, bestowing great care, but the boy was rather unusual. The only time he had cried loudly was at birth. After that he laughed but never cried, not even when he was hungry, and slept for very long periods, longer than other infants his age.

Looked well after by his mother he soon turned three years old but to everyone's dismay didn't utter a word.

They waited patiently but when after turning four he didn't start speaking, they began to suspect that he was dumb. Doctors, vaidyas, astrologers and holy men, all were consulted.

The doctors said his speech centre in the brain was probably affected and there was nothing much that could be done. The vaidyas were of the opinion that there was an imbalance of humors and gave him medicines which didn't seem to work.

The astrologers came out with their usual jargon of planetary positions and zodiac signs in his horoscope and suggested strange remedies that never worked.

Some holy men said they would pray to the goddess of speech but the goddess didn't seem to cooperate.

One wandering ascetic who came to beg for alms examined him closely and said that the devas, gods from a certain realm, have chosen him to do some work and that he would speak when they allowed him to.

It was too fantastic a theory and nobody believed him but to everyone's surprise he started speaking in clear sentences the day he turned five, as if he had been studying Malayalam during the years of silence.

Lalitha was very happy and she got him admitted to the local school; Kitcchu hated school but went reluctantly to make his mother happy.

By then he had developed into a sturdy, healthy and fair-complexioned boy, tall for his age and different from the other children of his age.

When the others played, or did their homework, he preferred to sit alone on the veranda and stare at the sky, watching the twinkling stars and other heavenly bodies. He was beyond a doubt convinced that different kinds of beings lived in worlds up above. He imagined them to possess human-like and sometimes non-human features.

The *asura*s, *deva*s, *kinnara*s, *rakshasa*s, *gandharva*s and their deeds his mother read out to him from the Puranas were realities as far as he was concerned. He felt he would meet them sometime.

In school the teachers considered him dull and dimwitted. He had little capacity to memorize and he evinced no interest in what was going on in the classroom. Many a time, he was caught staring out of the window at the trees and distant paddy fields and still more distant peaks of the Maruthwa mountains. Some day he thought to himself, he would go there. Perhaps there were caves there which the other-worldly beings visited. Repeated punishment neither improved his memorization skills nor deterred him from staring out of the window.

He somehow scraped through his exams in his next year in school, but the teachers noticed that his skills in mathematics and music had improved beyond expectation. The music teacher told his mother that her son would probably turn out to be a musical prodigy. He had an uncanny knack of learning ragas and manipulating the frequency of his voice to astonishingly high and low octaves.

The maths teacher confessed he couldn't understand how he suddenly started with the multiplication and division of large numbers with such ease considering his incapacity to memorize the multiplication tables.

* * *

The observers were happy with the state of affairs. Information was passed on to their supervisors in planet Swarga. The scientists were consulted. It was decided that they would merely watch till the boy turned eight. Meanwhile, the observers were told to prepare the caves, particularly the one in the centre for actually contacting and activating specific centres in the brain. They were familiar with the Maruthwa mountains. In the past, it had served as a landing pad for their aerial vehicles. A hundred years ago, a humanoid had been contacted and prepared for a certain mission. This was going to be the next.

* * *

Meanwhile, life went on for Kitcchu. He was given to long periods of solitude and occasional episodes of marathon, solo singing sessions. He also learnt to play the mridangam. But unlike children of his age he preferred solitude and disliked social or family gatherings and he loved the simple vegetarian food his mother cooked for him.

A few days after he turned eight, Kitcchu was filled with this incredible desire to walk to the Maruthwa mountains. It was a Sunday and just after his midday meal, he slipped away, not informing his mother or his aunt who lived with them.

It took him about an hour to reach the foot of the mountain. He looked up at the peak and on a sudden impulse, started climbing. His bare feet hurt but he continued to climb for over three hours. It looked like the path had been cleared of thorny bushes and rocks and he trekked up the mountain path along the trail, holding on to the branches of trees and stumbling sometimes but with no thought of giving up.

Tired and exhausted he finally reached a flat surface that seemed to have been hewn out of the rock. He realized that he had almost reached the peak. Kitcchu stretched himself on the flat surface and decided to take some rest before climbing any more. The sky looked closer than he had ever seen. Sitting up after a few minutes, he looked at the horizon. The sun was beginning to set, it would get dark soon. The wind was starting to turn cold.

It was then that he noticed a crevice on the side of the massive rock in front of which he had been lying down, barely large enough to squeeze through. In the excitement to explore what lay inside, all thoughts of the fast descending night and the fear of not being able to get back home were thrown to the wind.

Kitcchu got up and let himself in with a little effort. Inside all was dark but soon a faint blue light appeared from the roof of what he now noticed was a large cavern hewn out of the rock. The light turned a little stronger and Kitcchu saw three wooden stools on the floor and what looked like a tunnel at one end of the cavern.

Two white-clad beings as tall as an average human being came in from the tunnel-like opening.

Kitcchu felt no fear even though he noticed that their bodies weren't solid but almost translucent. Even the white, loose garments they wore were translucent. Their faces were beautiful in a feminine way. Their voices, when they spoke, were soft and musical.

'Welcome to our special place, Kitcchu,' they said in unison. Then they sat on the stools and gestured to Kitcchu to sit on the remaining stool.

One of them spoke. It was in the mixed Tamil–Malayalam dialect which people in that area spoke. Kitcchu, surprisingly, understood every word.

'Do you realize,' said the being who sat before him, 'that we come from the planet called Swarga and have chosen you for our work of bringing peace to this earth we call Bhuloka?'

'Yes, I think I do,' Kitcchu said.

'So, we made sure that physical conditions are created so that your mother would give birth to you while standing. Your head hit the ground and that part of the brain in humanoids that keeps their minds confined to mere three-dimensional thinking was shut off by the impact. Now, like us, you can think in four or five dimensions.'

'Yes,' said Kitcchu, 'I see that now.'

'Good. We have been watching over you. The earth, Bhuloka, is in the grip of anger and violence. If we don't step up and do something, it will be destroyed like many other civilizations in the past. All it requires is for a crazy, angry political leader to press the nuclear button. It would be hundred times more than the Hiroshima–Nagasaki disaster. This whole world and the wonderful civilization that has been built up painstakingly over the years will be reduced to ashes in no time.

'We have to prevent this, stop them before it's too late.

'We experimented before many times but the asuras and rakshasa beings of the planet called *Naraga* and diluted our efforts though they could not entirely nullify them.

'The first one who taught the knowledge of sound was Viwaswan who came from *Surya loka*. He made sure it was hidden in a secret language known only to the initiates in the great Sama Veda, the Veda of music and acoustics. The key was lost over the years.

'Krishna, the great being from the *Vaikunta* planet, revived it to some extent and although non-violence was emphasized in the Gita which he taught, very few understood the song of the Lord of Vaikunta, the Gita.

'Krishna himself had to side with the Pandava humanoids to fight the Kaurava humanoids controlled by the beings of Naraga planet who were trying to steal the secrets of the power of sound.

'Krishna taught the warrior race, Kshatriyas, the secret of sound, music and the sacred sound called Om. But they were so preoccupied with administrative matters and waging defensive wars to protect their subjects that the knowledge was lost and their descendants failed to learn it.

'Patanjali, the great writer of the yoga sutras, taught the science to a select few but they couldn't find worthy inheritors. So, it was lost again.

'We then taught great beings like the Buddha and a few more but they stressed on the philosophical and religious teachings more, quite aware that compassion was a prerequisite to learn this science. Since they were fully involved in this aspect of compassion, the science of sound was not given the importance it deserved. So, again, the techniques were lost.

'We tried Pythagoras, the great Greek mathematician and philosopher, who developed the theory of "the music of the spheres" which is a part of our teachings. He was instructed by our initiates in Egypt and Kashmir in India but the average humanoid brain wasn't equipped to practise the techniques.

'Several others were taught and tried—founders of religion, founders of the great kirtan movements and so on—but two factors contributed to the failure of the general public to learn this ancient science of acoustics; one was too much emotionalism and two, the humanoid brain was not yet ready for it.

'Now the time has come when a good percentage of humanoid brain and the cerebrospinal system is ready to receive and bring about results.'

There was a pause after which Kitcchu said, 'Understood.'

The other one who had been silent till now spoke.

'So now, we have you and if you agree, we can begin the process.'

'Yes, I do,' said Kitcchu.

'It is time we started seriously because the only humanoid who knew the secrets and belonged to an ancient family of Sama Veda chanters in Andhra Pradesh passed away three days ago. You need to help the Bhuloka you live in.

'This means you'll have to come once a week at night, Monday night to be precise, and spend several hours learning the theory and practice of the great science of *Pranava*, *Swara* and *Shabda*.

'Are you willing to do that?'

'Yes.'

'Okay, enough for the day then. It's dark now, half an hour past midnight. You won't be able to find the way back home so we'll drop you quietly. You can share your experiences with your mother, swear her to secrecy and take permission to visit us as scheduled.'

Kitcchu was then asked to get into an electric blue whirling disc-shaped object parked outside the cave. A door opened at the top and closed as soon as he entered. The disc started moving soundlessly.

* * *

Meanwhile, Lalitha had alerted the villagers that her son had gone for a walk and not returned. Search parties were organized but to no avail. Finally, the village sarpanch headed to the town to inform the police.

Lalitha couldn't sleep. She was lying in her bed, wide awake, staring at the roof and every once in a while looking out of the window anxiously. 'God! What's happened to my dear Kitcchu? Where did he go?' Her mind started wondering about all the possibilities. 'Could it be the leopard that was spotted a few miles away near Maruthwa hills? Or did he go swimming in the river and drown? Perhaps he'll return in the morning . . .' She promised to herself she would visit the nearby shrine of Hanuman and offer twenty bags of rice if he returned safe and sound.

A bluish light attracted her attention outside the window. A large shimmering blue disc silently glided down to the earth. The top opened and someone got out.

Lalitha sprung up. Could that be Kitcchu? What's that strange thing he stepped out of? 'No, no,' she said to herself. 'Perhaps the longing to see my son is making me see things.'

There was a knock at the door. She ran and opened it. There stood Kitcchu, her son. She hugged him and cried, 'O Kitcchu, you have come back! I knew you would, my son! I was praying to Hanuman-ji for your safety. What was that blue thing?'

She looked out of the door. There was nothing.

Could she have imagined all that? But then, Kitcchu was real. She held his hand, shut the door and took him into the bedroom.

'Where did you go, son? Are you hungry? What can I get you?'

'No,' said Kitcchu. 'I am not hungry. Will tell you everything tomorrow, I am tired now.'

Lalitha did not insist and let him rest. 'Come, my darling, come and sleep next to your Amma. You look so tired. Tell me everything in the morning.'

Holding each other, the mother and son fell asleep, a deep dreamless sleep.

* * *

The observers sent in their report, 'All okay. Things are fine. Arrangements have been made. *Swaha.*'

* * *

In the morning, Kitcchu related everything that had happened to his mother while eating his breakfast of idlis and chutney.

She took some time to process and finally spoke after a few minutes. 'So, let me get this straight, you will go once a week to Maruthwamalai. Spend the night and come back in the morning. I am to keep your nocturnal visits a secret.'

'Yes, Amma.'

'In any case, even if I had said these things, nobody would have believed me. They would have thought you have gone completely crazy, or I have, or both of us have! But I trust you, Kitcchu, my son.'

She kissed him on his forehead and the matter was settled.

***

Every Monday night Kitcchu went to the caves and was dropped back home in the *vimana*. The course he had agreed to was intensive.

His studies included the text called *Vimana Adhikara* and the ancient parts of the Sama Veda, no longer available to the public. He learnt for instance that even the great Albert Einstein was dyslexic and, to a great extent, owed his genius to music. He was an accomplished musician himself and it was his imagination more than cold logic that led him to the amazing theory of relativity.

For seven years, the lessons went on every week without fail. By then, he had compiled his scientific thesis on the theory of sound and its practical application to create advanced weapons that could protect nations by creating an impenetrable armour or *kavacha* that could withstand even nuclear-powered missiles. He learnt applications of sound energy to defuse atomic bombs from a distance of several miles and thus prevent the destruction and total annihilation of the human race.

He was taught the secret of melodies by which the human brain could be freed of violence and made peaceful. A similar experiment had previously been tried in the so-called Silly Sixties by the peaceniks but ended in failure because of drug abuse. The world was also not prepared yet to understand.

He was taught that the theory that sound cannot travel in a vacuum needed to be re-examined. Certain sounds called *Bijas*, seed sound, could not only travel in a vacuum, *shunya*, but could indeed create tremendous energy when the proper equipment was used. The silent vimana in which he was dropped home after every lesson worked on this principle.

He also learnt that all this knowledge had to wait for several years before breaking into the consciousness of a majority of human beings.

On one of his nocturnal visits they fixed electrodes to certain parts of his cerebrum and cerebellum, and passing a mild electric current, activated certain centres including the pineal gland.

With that, he could see sound frequencies in a pictoral form and hear sounds that originated from planets hundreds of light years away.

When he turned fourteen he completed his thesis. They, the elders of Swarga realm, helped him to submit his thesis to Yale University. It was titled 'The Theory of the Power of Sound and Its Applications' (TPSA).

During these years, Kitcchu had somehow managed to scrape through his exams and narrowly cleared his high school.

Then, tragedy struck. His mother died of a sudden brain haemorrhage. It was a terrible thing to happen and broke Kitcchu, but it also freed him from all bondage.

For a short while, his aunt came to stay in the home and look after him but then the observers brought the news that Professor Joseph Steiner had accepted his thesis and had invited him to join Yale as a research scholar—the youngest student he had worked with.

All arrangements were made by the observers and Kitcchu went to Yale. For three years, Prof. Steiner and Kitcchu worked together on the TPSA project.

When the thesis was published, the Nobel Prize for Peace and Physics was awarded jointly to Kitcchu and Prof. Joseph Steiner.

That's when the world came to know of this genius; a young Indian who, in childhood, was dyslexic, suffered from attention deficiency and lacked even the capacity to memorize simple words or tables; he was in fact considered a dull-witted idiot.

But after three days of receiving the Nobel Prize, Kitcchu disappeared. The police could not solve the mystery. Various rumours floated around, among them was the theory that he was kidnapped by the Russians or the Chinese. But nothing was ever proved.

The fact was that Kitcchu, after the work was done, volunteered to go to the Swarga realm to expand his consciousness further and reach perfection. Gladly, the rishis whisked him away in the silent vimana as light as a flower, therefore called the *Pushpa Vimana*.

* * *

It took a hundred years for world leaders and scientists to understand the work of Kitcchu of Suchindram and implement it. Scientists used the science of music to bring about peace and transform humanity on Planet Earth, or Bhuloka. Kitcchu become a legend. The world was saved from destruction.

The rishis of Swarga world were overjoyed that Bhuloka had been saved. After years of earth time, Kitcchu ascended the ladder of higher consciousness and became a rishi himself.

The Serpent Goddess

As Bagubhalan Singarayar, the zamindar of Chuthukuzi set out that fateful evening in his favourite turquoise blue 1915 Cadillac Touring Convertible, he didn't have the faintest hint of the danger that awaited him, nor did he anticipate this to be his last drive in the car he had inherited from his father.

Bagubhalan was named after his great-grandfather, the founder of the Chuthukuzi zamindari: a cruel and cunning man who was bestowed the title of *Singarayar*, 'lion among rulers' for beheading a rebellious courtier of the King Raja Kumara Chola and gifting the head to him in a decorated bamboo basket. He was then made the feudal chief of Chuthukuzi which consisted of six villages and 4000 acres of land.

When the Chola kingdom collapsed a hundred years ago, the zamindars became independent overlords and lived in great luxury.

The Chuthukuzi palace was an almost impregnable, fortified, stone structure surrounded by a moat with a number of crocodiles in it. Bagubhalan's grandfather was notorious for throwing erring subjects into the moat to be eaten alive by the crocodiles.

His father was a graduate from the Madurai Christian College who loved his scotch and ended many of the feudal cruelties. He was, however, inordinately fond of women and used his might to abduct any woman he set his eyes on, married or unmarried, from the villages under his domain to satisfy his sexual appetite. Under hushed tones, the villagers discussed his exploits and the sad story of the two women who committed suicide unable to bear the indignity of being raped in front of their husbands.

By the early 1900s, the absolute authority of the feudal chieftains was diluted but the subjects still feared the rich and influential zamindars which worked to Bagubhalan's advantage. One of the characteristics he inherited from his father was the almost insatiable hunger for other women, even though he was married to a beautiful dusky woman with lotus eyes.

He spent large sums of money to keep his sexual exploits secret. Vague rumours were afloat that he had raped a teenager who had gone to ask him for help in his hunting lodge twenty miles away which he often used to satisfy his sexual predilections, murdered her and thrown the body to the leopards when she threatened to complain to his wife. Nobody dared substantiate the rumours. The story that was presented to the public was that young Nallu was taken by a leopard.

Like his father, Bagubhalan enjoyed hunting wild boars and loved his Winchester rifle as much as the Cadillac Convertible he had inherited from his father, who died of a brain haemorrhage, when Bagubhalan was barely twenty-eight.

The traits he did not inherit from his father and grandfather before him were horse-riding and reverence for snakes, especially cobras.

Although in his bungalow in Ooty, a hill-station nearby, he had a stable of ten excellent horses that went to the annual races and won numerous awards, he disliked riding horses himself.

As for snakes, unlike his ancestors, he abhorred them. While his father and grandfather venerated cobras and built little shrines with granite images of the snakes which were worshipped regularly and would not dream of killing a real snake even if it wandered into their courtyard or inside the palace, Bagubhalan, after his father's death, promulgated an ordinance that the guards and other staff of the palace should kill any snakes, poisonous or non-poisonous, on sight.

More than that, he got all the little shrines built for snake-worship inside the campus and some outside destroyed. A large area of the surrounding woodlands was set on fire and hundreds of snakes were burnt to death.

This extreme phobia for snakes stemmed from a trauma he had gone through when he was five years old. A black cobra had managed to crawl into his bed one afternoon while he was trying to take a nap. His screams brought his father, mother and many of the staff to the bedroom but no one would dare kill the cobra for fear of the curse of the snake goddess. Frozen and petrified with fear he had to endure the terrible, hair-raising feel of the glistening snake, as it slithered all over his body, expecting it to strike at any moment. Luckily, it had crawled out of his bed, out of the room and into the courtyard.

Then and there, Bagubhalan had sworn that he would kill all the snakes in the premises and the neighbourhood, as soon as he inherited the zamindari. That he had been educated in a Christian missionary school in Madurai, helped in getting his mind rid of the idea that snakes were divine and had to be worshipped.

He went about it ruthlessly and systematically. The largest temple of the snake goddess *Naga Kanya* stood in what was now his hunting lodge surrounded by ten acres of thick forest. Hundreds of snakes were killed when he ordered the forest to be set on fire. The temple of the snake goddess was demolished and a luxurious one-bedroom hunting lodge where his henchmen brought him girls to feed his unending sexual hunger was built. It was here that Nallu was raped, killed and thrown to the leopards.

It was the same hunting lodge that Bagubhalan was heading to that evening.

At thirty-five, he was a tall and handsome man, his complexion as dark as his curly, black hair and following his father's and grandfather's custom had a thick upturned military moustache of the variety worn by Tamil warriors of yore.

Word had been sent to the caretaker Muthu, who lived in the outhouse near the luxurious hunting lodge, to keep the bedroom clean and ready for the chief. Bagubhalan liked to hunt in the night, with flashlights and searchlights that were mounted on the old four-wheel drive Willy's Jeep that was parked in the hunting lodge. Perhaps Muthu would find Bagubhalan a girl at night.

By the time he reached the lodge it was dark and had started raining. Muthu was waiting for him with the cook and the armed security guard. Bagubhalan was disappointed on two counts: One, the rain had increased. It was a thunderstorm, with blinding flashes of lightning and it was impossible to hunt under the circumstances; two, Muthu had failed to secure a woman for his pleasure. He uttered some vague excuse and it crossed Bagubhalan's mind that it was time to get rid of the fellow and get someone young, robust and enthusiastic. He let the thought pass for the moment.

Inside, the gas lamps were well lit, for electricity still hadn't found its way to Chuthukuzi and the warm fireplace offered welcome comfort on a wet and rainy day.

His favourite imported whisky, Johnnie Walker Black Label, was on the table beside the rocking chair by the fireplace.

He sat down on the rocking chair, poured himself a stiff drink and told Muthu he wasn't going back home in the heavy rain and would spend the night there. 'I need to talk to you, but we can do that in the morning. What has Joseph got for dinner?'

The cook Joseph said he had wild fowl roasted, rice and spicy *vattakulambu*.

'Great, now will you leave me alone?' He looked at the old clock. 'And Joseph, bring me the food in an hour's time. It's eight o'clock right now.'

When they left, he closed the door, latched it and went back to the chair. It was still raining heavily and the clouds rumbled. He could see the flashes of lightning from the glass-paned windows.

Bagubhalan sat by the fire, drank and thought about many things. For some reason, Nallu's sexy face and figure kept coming back to his mind, which was quite unusual. He thought he had wiped it out of his memory long ago. Perhaps he should have married her and kept her as his second wife. After all, his father had had three wives and his grandfather four.

As the old clock chimed nine, Joseph knocked. He opened the door for him. Joseph laid the food on the small circular rosewood dining table near the bed saying, 'Dinner is ready, *Ayya*,' and withdrew discreetly. 'Clear the table in the morning. Don't disturb me now,' Bagubhalan shouted after him.

After three straight whiskeys, he pulled the cane dining chair close to the table and had a hearty meal. Joseph was an excellent cook. The food was delicious.

Contented, he changed into a coloured lungi and cotton vest, used the washroom and made sure that the ventilator was properly closed—snakes could crawl in through ventilators—and came back to the bedroom.

Bagubhalan then turned off the main gaslight and lit the reading light. Since the snake episode of his childhood, he couldn't sleep without a light. He latched the door, and picked up Volume I of the works of Robert Ingersoll, the American atheist, from the bedside bookshelf and stretched himself on the bed.

Outside it was still raining. The thunder and lightning had reduced quite a bit. After a few pages he was on the verge of falling into a whisky-induced sleep when he thought he saw a shadow flit past the window on his right.

Bagubhalan clasped his hand on his Winchester rifle that he always kept beside the bed and shouted, 'Who's there?' No answer. Only silence, except for a soft rustling.

And then he heard the knock at the door. A gentle knock.

He cocked his rifle, and holding it in his right hand, walked to the door, unlocked the latch and opened the door just a little.

In the momentary flash of lightning, he discerned a female draped in a white sari, fully drenched by the rain.

For a second, fear gripped him. He tightened his grip on the rifle. Nallu! No, it couldn't be. He had strangled her with his own hands . . .

One more flash of lightning and he relaxed. This wasn't Nallu. The heavy brass earrings were worn by tribal women and she was extremely dark complexioned. 'I am shivering with cold, Ayya. Please let me in?' she pleaded. 'I can't find my way back home at this hour. I'll leave in the morning.'

'Come in,' he said, stepping aside to let her in and bolted the door. He walked to the bed and turned the reading light brighter.

Except for her long black, abundant hair tied in a knot on top of her head, which was unusual for tribals who had short hair, she looked every inch a tribal girl. The heavy brass earrings, the dark and shining round face, large intense eyes, attractive lips that reminded him of a famous African-American model's picture he had seen in a foreign magazine somewhere, and the voluptuous figure draped in a sari which, drenched in the rain, had turned diaphanous. For a minute he just stood staring at her speechless, wondering what a bonanza chance had thrown into his bedroom. 'What's your name, girl?

'Kathiri . . .'

Kathiri meant scissors. Tribals had strange names and he loved her voice.

'Came to collect firewood, Ayya,' she continued. 'It became dark and with the rain and thunder I got lost. Couldn't find my way home. I am scared of thunder and lightning. I can sleep on the floor tonight. I'll go back early at daybreak tomorrow.'

Bagubhalan was more than pleased, he was excited. This was much more than what Muthu could have provided. He pulled out a towel and a white dhoti from the cupboard and handed it over to her. 'Go into the bathroom, rub yourself dry, wrap this dhoti around yourself and come back. Yes, you can sleep here.'

Bagubhalan quickly poured himself another shot of whisky, drank it up and sat on his bed, waiting for her. If she resisted, he knew what to do. Come what may, he must have her. The heat of intense passion made his body tremble. The hunger had to be satiated.

The white dhoti barely hid her curves as she stood before him. For the first time he noticed the snake-shaped heavy bronze anklets she wore and for some reason that excited him even more.

'You will be sleeping with me in my bed,' he said. 'Not on the floor.'

'Whatever you say, Ayya,' she said coyly.

The sideways glance she gave him with her fish-shaped eyes was an invitation to take her to bed. Quietly she climbed into the bed and lay beside him.

Bagubhalan lost no time. He clasped her in a hot embrace and kissed her on her cheeks. She laughed loudly. It sounded like the ringing of the temple bell. 'Which temple had he heard this sound before?' Her legs and arms were wrapped tightly around his body. And then he remembered . . . 'The temple of the snake goddess, the one he . . .'

'Kiss me on my lips, Ayya,' she whispered. Her skin had an intoxicating fragrance like the flowers of the night queen.

Baghubalan closed his eyes and kissed her and her tongue entered his mouth. Burning with passion, he was trying to enter her. The lower part of her body wriggled in a strange way. The slithering ascended to the upper part of the body. Which reminded him of the cobra when he was a boy, all alone in his bedroom.

Bagubhalan's hair stood on end. The tongue inside his mouth was now forked and he heard her hissing close to his right ear. Passion was replaced by a terrible fear and his body went cold. He opened his eyes and shivered from head to toe.

There was no tribal damsel. She had turned into a black cobra, the largest he had ever seen. Its black, shining eyes were staring at him. Tongue darting and hood expanded, it was ready to strike. And then the scissor mark in the hood, *Kathiri*, which only cobras possessed.

He wanted to scream but his vocal chords failed him. He wanted to rise and run but he was paralysed with fear.

The shimmering black serpent struck him on his neck, precisely on his carotid artery, slithered down and bit him on his penis. Then it slid down the bed and sat on the floor to make sure her victim died.

Bagubhalan died within a few minutes. Even before the poison had its effect he had a massive cardiac arrest.

* * *

In the morning, Joseph the cook and Muthu the caretaker knocked at the door. After knocking for long and getting no answer, they moved to the side and looked in through the glass panes of the French window. What they saw convinced them that everything was not all right with their lord. His mouth was open and his naked body was lying in a strange position as if he had tried to grapple with something. They didn't see the cobra which sat on the other side of the bed.

After a short discussion among themselves they decided to break open the door. With the help of the security guard they broke the door open and entered. One look and they knew he was dead. The marks where the serpent fangs had entered his neck were clearly visible, swollen and dark blue.

It was then they saw the cobra and froze. It was a black cobra, the biggest they had ever seen with a distinct scissor mark on its expanded hood. The serpent quietly slithered away and exited from the front door.

Later they saw the serpent-shaped brass anklets among the sheets and sensed the strange fragrance of the night queen, the favourite flower of the female cobra.

The doctor came from Madurai, the nearest city, and declared him dead. Cause of death: snakebite and cardiac arrest.

From Muthu and Joseph, the villagers learnt about the queen of snakes, the *Naga kanya* who had avenged the destruction of her temple and the killing of hundreds of snakes.

The hunting lodge was abandoned forever and soon crumbled. The villagers built a small temple for the snake goddess and worshipped her image regularly.

The Homecoming

Kondanda Shivanna Thimappa was born with a silver spoon in his mouth. A coffee-gilded silver spoon would be a better way to put it. He was the only child of Kondanda Raghunatha Thimappa and Kaveri who owned 800 acres of coffee and pepper plantations in Somwarpet, in the Coorg district of Karnataka. A little before the Land Ceiling Act was promulgated by the government, he had turned his holdings into a family-held private limited company and named his estate Kaveri Estates after his wife.

The richer and more influential families of Coorg were proud of their martial origins and being tough warriors suited to the hill terrain of Coorg, they had helped the British soldiers fight the Muslim ruler of Mysore, Tipu Sultan.

From those days, the British categorized them as a 'martial race' and sent many of the young men to Sandhurst Military School to be trained as officers. One of Shivanna's paternal uncles was a Sandhurst-trained officer who later on rose to be a general and commander-in-chief of the Indian Army.

The English also loved the Kodavas for their love of pork and whisky. The upper class among the Kodavas were completely anglicized except for their religion. They were staunch Hindus.

Shivanna, therefore, lived in a large English bungalow with an old Andaman teakwood ceiling and marble floors, in the centre of a sprawling lush green coffee estate waited on by maids, cooks, butlers, drivers and other paraphernalia that belonged typically to old English country houses.

Shivanna, from his childhood, was a quiet, meditative boy and loved sitting under the big banyan tree, doing nothing in particular and spending time with the cows in the cowshed. He also loved to sit by the stream that flowed through their estate.

As he grew up into a young man, it was noticed that when he came home for vacations from Madras where he studied in the Madras Christian College—a prestigious hundred-year-old college—he was reading the works of Swami Vivekananda and other books on Yoga and Hindu philosophy. He became a vegetarian and unlike most young men his age, didn't frequent the bars that abound in Coorg. Some of his friends considered him a misfit, for the heart and soul of Coorg was pork and the endless flow of beer and whisky. Shivanna would sit in a corner sipping grape juice. Nevertheless, they appreciated the fact that he was very knowledgeable when it came to Hindu philosophy and ancient Indian culture and above all that he was a real friend-in-need and would go out of his way if they needed help. They had playfully nicknamed him *Saami*, a term used for holy men.

His parents were a little worried that he wasn't fitting into the stereotyped image of a young Coorgi boy but then, they were happy that he was very good at academics, extremely respectful towards elders and was always pleasantly mannered.

Then one day, just as he turned twenty, their happiness was suddenly shattered by a rude shock. Shivanna suddenly disappeared. He had gone for a walk and didn't return.

The security guard at the main gate said that he had gone out of the estate at around 6 p.m. He said he was going for a walk.

At 10 p.m., he hadn't returned. His parents telephoned his friends. No one knew his whereabouts. Raghunath Thimappa stayed awake till midnight. 'Perhaps he is with your sister in Napoklu, who he is very fond of. She doesn't have a telephone. He'll come in the morning,' he tried to reassure himself and went to sleep.

His mother Kaveri couldn't sleep till four in the morning. When they woke up at dawn, he still hadn't come back. There were no cell phones those days. Raghunath took out his car and drove to Madikeri, where he lodged a complaint with the superintendent of police, who was his good friend. Then he met all the people who he thought might have some information. Sadly, no one knew. He returned to the estate disheartened.

Kaveri was weeping uncontrollably. Her sister was with her, consoling her. Unable to bear the situation, Raghunath made himself a planter's punch, a strong rum-based cocktail, sat in an easy chair on the porch and sipped his drink, lost in thought.

The large estate and the bungalow looked kind of blank to him. His mind wandered in all sorts of directions, questions running through his mind. Who would inherit all this? His only hope had just disappeared. Was he alive? Did he die of a snakebite? Or some fatal accident? As he downed the second glass, a thought occurred to him that perhaps he had gone to some ashram and might eventually come back. Raghunath had lost his apetite and fell asleep in the easy chair without eating a meal.

Kaveri woke him up. 'Shall I give you some food?'

'No,' he said. 'Not hungry. Did you eat?'

'No, I am not hungry either. Let's go and sleep. I'm very tired. Have vowed to offer 1 lakh rupees and 100 coconuts to *Igguthappa*. Shiva will surely come back,' she said hopefully and they went to sleep.

Two days passed and they continued to wait for Shivanna. On the morning of the third day, the postman delivered a letter addressed to Kaveri and Raghunath. It was in Shivanna's handwriting.

'Dear Mummy and Dad, I'm leaving to be on my own in search of the spiritual Truth which our ancient scriptures describe. You have been wonderful parents to me and I am grateful to you. Please forgive me for this. No need to search for me. God will protect me.'

It was indeed a terrible shock to his parents. Kaveri couldn't stop crying for many days and needed medication to sleep. Raghunath, shocked but not surprised, for the first time in his life wept loudly as he was going through the family album.

The only thought that helped to restore them to near normalcy in about a year was that Shiva was alive. Perhaps he would come back.

Kaveri hung up a lovely photograph of her son along with the pictures of other deities in the puja room, offered flowers and lit the oil lamp every evening.

Raghu downed his sorrows by immersing himself in estate work, playing golf at the Madikeri Downs Golf Course and consumed liberal quantities of planter's punch.

At the end of the day, Kaveri would stand at the door hoping that Shiva would have changed his mind and would walk in any moment. She gave up the practice after a year. With no sign of Shiva, life continued the same way in Kaveri Estate.

In the second year after Shiva's disappearance, Raghu was diagnosed with liver complications and kidney malfunction. He passed away within a month of hospitalization. Relatives and friends wondered what would happen to the estate.

They were in for a surprise.

Kaveri decided to take charge of her estate. 'My son will come back sometime,' she said, fully certain of that reality. 'I am confident. Till then I am going to run the estate on his behalf.'

The manager, Mr Thomas, swore upon God that he would assist to the best of his capacity till 'Shivan Kunju' as he called him, returned. He said he prayed to Jesus every day. Surely, sometime he would return.

Six years passed.

* * *

On the day he had walked out of home, Shiva went straight to Madikeri and boarded a bus to Mysore. He had to get as far away from Madikeri as possible.

In Mysore, he bought himself a travel-bag, some clothes, sweater and a notebook, and boarded a bus to Bangalore. Money wasn't a problem. His pocket money which he had saved for one year came in handy.

He got himself a train ticket from Bangalore to New Delhi. He had done some research. There was a large ashram on the outskirts of Delhi called the Vedanta Seva Mission. He reached the ashram after three days of travel and met the acharya, Swami Nirgunanandagiri, and was admitted as a brahmachari inmate. The ashram was located on the banks of the Yamuna River and Shiva loved meditating on the ghats. Everything went well for some time. But soon he discovered that they stressed more on service than meditation. The acharya said only unselfish service of the underprivileged would purify the mind. He was given a mantra to chant but that was that.

Shiva yearned to learn the higher techniques of meditation and find the Truth. He was not happy with the state of affairs as they stood. One day, he took permission from the head of the ashram and proceeded towards the Himalayas.

Spending time in various ashrams in Haridwar and Rishikesh and further up in Uttarkashi and Gangotri, after five years one summer he reached Badrinath and found himself a small kutir (hut) not far from the Alaknanda River.

That the acharya of the Vedanta Seva Mission had initiated him into the life of a religious service and given him the name of Shivaprasad Giri, helped him to seek free accommodation and food from the *Anna Kshetras*.

All this while, he had studied many religious texts and learnt to practise yoga from a number of teachers, but found no teacher whom he felt like accepting as his spiritual guru.

There were sadhus of all kinds, the rich ones with thousands of followers, the learned ones, the showmen who practised magic, the yoga experts, the clever business types, who in the garb of religious mendicants sold their wares to unsuspecting foreigners seeking short cuts to enlightenment, and of course the cannabis addicts who believed they had reached an exalted state.

None of these appealed to him and having read the teachings of Ramana Maharshi, he decided to travel the spiritual path alone, all by himself, living in solitude close to the snow-clad peaks of Badrinath.

He would often come across sadhus on his solitary walks towards Vasundhara falls beyond Mana, the last Indian village on the Indo-China border. But no one interested him or attracted his attention.

It was in Badrinath, as he sat near the Alaknanda River, far away from the tourist circuit, past the Vyasa Guha, that for the first time he heard a voice say, 'Go back home, Shiva. You'll find what you seek right there. Your mother is alone now. Go back before she dies heartbroken. Satisfy her desire to see you. You'll find God in your heart.'

Shiva looked around. He was shaken by the message. Who did the voice belong to? There was no one around. Was his mind playing tricks?

For three days, every morning and evening, the same musical voice spoke. The message was the same. Shiva was convinced it was not his imagination. He decided he would return and see what the situation at home was. For the first time he felt remorse at having been responsible for his mother's grief. If things were okay back home, he decided he would return to the Himalayas.

Problem was that he had no money now but with the help of the chief priest of Badrinath, a Sanskrit scholar with whom he had developed a strong bond, he managed to borrow enough money to pay for his travel.

And so, six years after he had left Coorg, Shiva returned to Kaveri Estate one evening at 6.00 p.m. In Mysore, he had gone to a barber shop, had a neat haircut and shaved off his beard and moustache. His hair and beard had grown wild and he didn't want to shock his already grief-stricken mother. He had also changed into grey pants and a white slack shirt he had purchased from there.

As he entered the main gate, the security guard saw him and shouted with excitement, 'Shivappa, you have come back! You are here! Let me take you to Amma.'

'No, you stay here,' Shiva said kindly. 'I want to surprise her. Where is Thomas uncle?'

'He is on leave for two days . . .' said the guard and before he could tell him that his father was no more, Shiva walked to the door of their English-style bungalow. He entered the house and went straight to the puja room. He knew that's where his mother would be at that time.

He was right. She had lit the lamps and was praying. He was surprised to see his own photograph and his father's added to the deities in the room.

Quietly, he went close to his mother and whispered, 'Mummy . . .'

Kaveri couldn't believe her eyes. They hugged each other and wept for what seemed to be forever. After a while they sat in the drawing room and talked. Kaveri sent away all kitchen and estate staff who had gathered to see Shiva. 'Your father passed away two years after you left. He put up a brave front but couldn't take it,' she said, reminiscing sadly.

She continued, 'Are you okay, my son? You won't go away now, I hope? You can do all that you want to do here, meditation, yoga, puja,' she continued breathlessly. 'If you want we can build a small cottage for your solitude in the estate near the river. Just don't go away. Please don't go away. I won't trouble you about getting married. Just be here with Mummy. Okay?'

Shiva promised her he would not go away. 'I'll be with you, Mummy,' he said. 'I'll look after you and the estate. I love you,' he consoled her.

They hugged each other again.

And so life went on as usual in the estate. Mr Thomas, the manager, taught Shiva the intricacies of running a coffee and pepper estate.

A lot of changes came about the house and the estate. Shiva, with his mother's cooperation, turned the kitchen vegetarian. No meat, no fish, no eggs. He enjoyed *akki roti* though, along with chickpea masala.

On the bank of the stream that flowed through the estate, Shiva built a nice little room which he frequently used for meditation. He had always been fond of cows and so, the dairy was spruced up and more cows were added.

Shiva spent many hours looking after the cows, feeding them and occasionally, sometimes even milking them himself.

* * *

It happened one morning in the cowshed so inconspicuously that Shiva didn't realize the significance of the encounter.

One of the workers in the dairy had quit his job two days ago and Shiva was helping in milking the cows when the estate manager Thomas came, accompanied by a young man clad in a brown sleeveless vest and a blue lungi. He looked around twenty, had a clean-shaven head and face, almost charcoal black in complexion and was barefoot.

Thomas said, 'I know this boy's uncle. He is a Malayalee. He has has worked in a dairy farm in Kozhikode for two years. I thought he could be useful here. His uncle says he is a hard worker and loves being with cows.'

'What's your name?' Shiva asked.

'Appan.'

'Will you be okay living here? Do you have parents? Are you married?'

'I am single. An orphan, I lost my parents. I'm fond of cows, I like them very much,' he responded.

'Milk that cow,' said Shiva.

Appan went up to the black and white cow Karpi, who usually didn't like strangers, patted her, spoke to her soothingly and milked her with ease.

'Okay, let him stay,' said Shiva. 'When can you join work?'

'Now,' he responded, to Shiva's surprise.

'Clothes?'

'I have them here,' he said, pointing to a gunny sack he had placed outside the cowshed.

'All right,' said Shiva and walked out of the cowshed accompanied by Thomas.

'He can live in the servant quarters with two other chaps who work in the dairy,' said Thomas. 'When I told him he will get food and two thousand rupees, he seemed quite satisfied.'

'Okay,' said Shiva. 'Let's try him out for a while.'

And so Appan settled down in Kaveri Estate.

He worked hard. The cowshed was kept spick and span and he had a way with cows. They seemed to love him. Shiva's mother liked him too and wondered why he hardly talked when he came for his meals with other workers in the dining area in the backyard of the house. He was gentle with the other estate staff and had an innocent smile. Shiva liked him too. It looked like Appan was going to settle down long term.

Then one day, something strange happened. Chellamma, the wife of one of the estate workers, came to see Shiva and said she wanted to talk to him about some strange goings-on regarding Appan.

She said, 'My husband and I noticed that Appan would often go to the cowshed at night. We wondered why. One day we asked him and he said he loved to sleep amongst cows, especially in summer. "Fresh air," he said and that he liked the smell of cows.

'After two months we became curious and decided to investigate.

'One full-moon night, we followed him, surreptitiously hiding behind the bushes, this is what we saw. He tied two stout lengths of rope to the rafter of the cowshed and turned them into loops. Then he stood straight up on his arms and pushed his feet into the loops. Then he folded his arms across his chest and hung upside down with his eyes closed.

We waited for some time and he continued to hang upside-down. The fear of talking to someone who seemed to be doing an utterly crazy thing prevented us from going close or asking him anything. What if he assaulted us? So we tiptoed away,' she finished.

'Did you ask him later?'

'Yes, we did and he said something quite crazy. He said he liked sleeping upside down and laughed. "Don't come sneaking again," he said.'

'I'll talk to him and try to figure out,' said Shiva calmly, but finding this all very strange.

Nanu, Chellamma's husband, said, 'Pappan, who sleeps in the quarters next to him, says, Appan talks in a strange language at night and often laughs loudly.'

'Okay. I will check,' Shiva said, thinking hard as he dismissed her.

A strange thought occurred to Shiva. What if this chap was actually a yogi? Some Hatha yogis were known to hang themselves upside down as part of their yogic practice.

When Appan spoke to him on the day he had come in with Thomas, Shiva had wondered if the voice sounded familiar. Suddenly it struck him. Was it the same voice he had heard in Badrinath that said, 'Go back home.' Or was he just overthinking?

'Far-fetched,' he said to himself. 'Your imagination is running riot, Shiva. It's your intense desire to find a guru.'

Whatever it was, Shiva resolved that he would investigate. It was premature to speak to Appan. He wondered if the best plan of action would be to follow him one night and see for himself.

On the next full-moon night, a little after midnight, armed with a powerful flashlight, mainly to make sure he didn't step on a snake, for quite a number of cobras lived in the estate, Shiva tiptoed towards the cowshed.

As he neared the cowshed, he switched off the flashlight. The moonlight was bright enough to look around.

He hid himself behind the lantana bushes that grew near the cowshed in a semi-circle and waited. From there he could see the inside of the cowshed clearly.

One of the calves sensed some movement behind the bushes and mooed in alarm but soon became silent. Only the crickets went about their loud, rhythmic chant. The barn owl hooted close by, sounding almost human.

Shiva must have waited for about five minutes when he saw him walking rapidly towards the cowshed. Appan was naked except for a *kaupina*, loincloth, and his black body glistened in the moonlight—he seemed to be laughing and muttering to himself.

Entering the cowshed, he patted the brown and white calf which stayed calm, walked to the right-hand corner of the shed and squatted on his gunny bag.

Shiva was surprised that none of the twelve cows seemed alarmed by this midnight intrusion and remained unusually quiet. But he assumed that was probably because, as Chellamma informed him, he did this often.

It was what happened after this that sent shivers up Shiva's spine. In a shrill voice, Appan shouted, 'Hey you, *sarpas* hiding in your holes, come here and enjoy. Appan is waiting for you.'

Soon one snake and then another and another . . . around a dozen cobras, big and small, black and brown, slithered into the cowshed and wrapped themselves around Appan's body in different positions. The large black one around his neck and shoulders raised its hood and gently swayed.

Appan's face was lit with an ecstatic smile and he kept muttering something unintelligible, gently stroking the cobras. The cows showed no sign of alarm.

Shiva was sweating profusely and started shivering.

Appan said after a while, 'Go back, you sarpas. We will meet on the next full moon.'

To Shiva's astonishment, one by one the cobras slid off Appan's body and disappeared into the darkness.

When all of them had gone, Appan turned in the direction Shiva was hiding and said, 'Hey, Shivappa, hiding behind the bushes, come forward. You sought me in the Himalayas for so long. Now here I am, and you hide behind the bushes? Come out, you seeker.'

Shiva came out of his hiding place and hesitantly walked towards Appan. The intense fear that had taken hold of him had not entirely subsided. With faltering steps, he moved into the cowshed and stood facing Appan.

'Umph, you surely are a sincere spiritual seeker. See why I asked you to go back home? Now I have come to you,' Appan said, laughing loudly.

'Come, let's go to your cottage by the river.'

Appan led the way and Shivappa followed.

On the eastern bank of the stream that flowed through Kaveri Estate, stood the little kutir that Shivappa had built for his meditation. When they reached the kutir, Appan said, 'Now open the door.'

Shivappa opened the door and entered. The room was filled with the fragrance of jasmine. He wondered how because he hadn't left any jasmine flowers inside nor had he lit any incense.

Appan entered the tiny room and said, 'Sit down on your meditation mat.'

Shivappa sat down cross-legged.

'Now,' said Appan, 'don't ask me any questions. Keep your mouth shut and close your eyes.'

Shivappa obeyed.

Appan touched him softly at the point between the eyebrows and the crown of his head.

A warm and ecstasy-filled current moved up his spine. Beautiful lights appeared in his mind's eye. The current reached the crown of his head. The world disappeared. There was only the One ecstatic Self, free of all conditioning and personality. No Shiva, no Appan, only pure pulsating, all-pervading consciousness with no limitation. A spiritual orgasm that is a thousand times more intense than the sexual experience.

Shiva had arrived where he wanted to be all this while, the place he sought from within, the Truth he wanted to know of. The voice had said, 'Go home.' Indeed. He was home.

For many hours, Shiva was in unending bliss. The cock crowed three times outside and woke him up at dawn. But where was Appan, his guru, his guide? He was nowhere to be seen.

After he had recovered from his spiritual state, the search for Appan began. He couldn't be found anywhere. It seemed as if he had vanished without a trace.

Shivappa said to himself, 'He came for a purpose and now he is gone.'

Shivappa continued to live in the estate and look after it. He lead a simple saintly life, meditating and enjoying the bliss of his inner self and teaching those who would care to learn the way to a joyous spiritual life while still leading an outwardly normal life.

As life moved on, after his mother's death, Shivappa formed the Appan Karunya Trust which ran an old-age home for the poor and the destitute and taught the practice of meditation.

The Assassin

Ghulam Ali Matoo was handpicked by the chief of Pakistan's Inter-Services Intelligence (ISI) Brigadier Afzal Khan for this top-priority assassination codenamed Operation EIPM (Eliminate Indian Prime Minister).

Matoo fit the bill perfectly. A sharp shooter par-excellence, he had successfully accomplished two assassinations in his five years with the ISI. The first one was a high-ranking lieutenant general of the Indian Army in charge of counter-insurgency operations and the last one a high-profile operation in which an ex-prime minister of Pakistan had to be done off with because she was proving to be a threat to the Pakistan Army's totalitarian ambitions.

But more than that was the psychological factor. An ex-inspector of the J&K Police, known for his efficiency in dealing with insurgents, defected to the other side six years ago.

His defection was an emotion-filled story initiated by his love for his old friend Mustapha who had turned a terrorist. Ghulam Ali had gone to his ancestral home in Baramullah on a vacation with his wife Zarina and his brown-eyed four-year-old daughter Huma whom he loved more than anything in this world.

Someone knocked at his door late at night after his daughter and wife had gone to sleep. He opened the door carefully, not forgetting to take his revolver. These were dangerous times. He had information that Pakistan-sponsored terrorists could be in the locality. He wondered who it could be on this cold night.

A voice whispered hoarsely, 'It's me, Mustapha, your old friend.'

Ghulam Ali directed the beam of his flashlight at the face of the figure outside the door. He was wearing a woollen pheran and a monkey cap that covered most of his face except the eyes and nose.

Ghulam recognized the voice but to be doubly sure he quickly jerked up Mustapha's right sleeve. There it was, the litchi-sized heart he had tattooed himself with when he was in love with this doe-eyed Pandit girl in college.

'Come in,' said Ghulam Ali, 'and don't make any noise. My wife and daughter are fast asleep. They shouldn't wake up.'

Inside the house, they sat near the sigri. It was warm and comfortable. 'Shall I make you some kehwa? No? Okay, so tell me, what are you up to. Haven't seen you for years. How did you know I was here?'

Mustapha said, 'I came to seek protection, hide from the BSF soldiers who are looking for me. They have labelled me a terrorist but I am a jihadi fighting for Islam against these infidel Hindus.'

'Mustapha, I am a police officer and I don't agree with this nonsense. The Hindus are not our enemies. There are good and bad Muslims. They have brainwashed you. I suggest you surrender. Are you the one known to the NSA as *Dushman*? Number 3 on the list?'

'Yes,' said Mustapha. 'I don't agree with you. *You* have been brainwashed, not me. Anyway, they are after me. Can I please hide here for a day or two? Please, I beg you! They won't suspect I am here with you. Day after tomorrow I'll move out. Please, my friend.'

'Mustapha, what I should actually be doing is arrest you and inform the NSA but I can't bring myself to do it. I suggest you go right now before I change my mind. You have already killed a couple of soldiers, if my information is correct. I can't protect you. But yes, you indeed were my dearest friend once upon a time,' Ghulam said sorrowfully.

'If the BSF finds you and a gunfight ensues because I don't think you are in a mood to surrender, my wife's and my precious daughter's life will be in danger. Go, I beg you.'

From inside his pheran, Mustapha produced an AK-47. He pointed it at Ghulam Ali. 'You enemies of Allah, I hate you turncoats. Don't move! Put down your revolver and keep quiet. I am not leaving.'

Ghulam Ali clicked open the cover of a small silver pendant he wore on his neck on a silver chain and showed Mustapha the tiny photograph of his daughter Huma. 'Mustapha, this is the jewel of my heart. She sleeps inside next to my darling wife. If anything happens to them I will never forgive you. The BSF is sure to trace you here. Please go away, leave us alone. I have nothing against you.'

Before Mustapha could answer, the door burst open and two jawans of the BSF entered the house. 'Put down your guns!' they shouted, 'or we will shoot!'

Mustapha started shooting with his AK-47. Ghulam Ali tried to identify himself but nothing could be heard in the din. Zarina, hearing the loud noise, picked up her daughter and came into the room.

'Go flat on the floor!' shouted Ghulam Ali and, grabbing them, tried to duck behind the sofa. But it was too late. A bullet hit Zarina's chest and another went through little Huma's abdomen, pierced through her body all the way into the kitchen through the open door.

Ghulam Ali knew his wife and daughter were both dead. He rolled into the kitchen, opened the back door and ran into the darkness of the backyard.

He heard a command in the background. 'Shoot! There is someone there.' He ducked behind the old apple tree and fired with his revolver in the direction of the voice. Someone screamed and there was silence. Ghulam Ali scaled the wooden compound wall and ran into the night. The half-moon came out from behind the clouds. For the first time he realized he was wounded and bleeding profusely. His left shoulder had been hit. He was in excruciating pain but he kept running not knowing where he was heading. He saw an army patrol jeep parked near a shed. A voice said, 'Drop your gun.'

He knew there was no chance. There probably were more soldiers in the darkness. He dropped the gun and raised his hands.

An armed soldier in Indian Army uniform walked up to him. 'Come with us,' he said. 'You have been wounded badly.'

Two more soldiers in army fatigues appeared and took him into the jeep. The last words he heard before he fainted were, 'Assalaamualaikum. I am Colonel Majeed from the Pakistani Army, counter-intelligence. We know who you are. You are in safe hands.'

* * *

After a lengthy debriefing and Islamic indoctrination which could better be described as brainwashing, the Inter-Services Intelligence turned him into an India-hater and anti-Hindu zealot who believed that he had to take revenge and make the Indian government pay for the murder of his wife and dear daughter. Little did he know that the entire operation had been stage-managed by the ISI and the soldiers who had broken into his house were Pakistani soldiers in BSF uniforms.

Thus Ghulam Ali—codenamed SS (sharp shooter), with his burning hatred for India and sharp-shooting abilities further strengthened by intensive training in weapons— became the perfect choice for operation EIPM.

* * *

The National Security Advisor of the Government of India received a call from the chief of the RAW. 'Sir, we have information that the ISI is plotting a highly secret operation codenamed EIPM—Eliminate Indian Prime Minister. Our informant says a sharp-shooter has been identified to assassinate the PM at the inauguration of the Kartarpur Corridor.'

'That's close, next week. Do you have details of the assassin or assassins who have been chosen?'

'Seems to be a lone operator, sir. We are trying to identify him. We will get back to you the moment we know.'

'Okay, and have you shortlisted the team that will handle this from our side?'

'Roughly sir, but we will go into the operational procedure after having identified the assassin. We will get back to you.'

'It better be fast. We have just a week.'

'Yes, sir.'

In two days, they had the information. Ghulam Ali, codenamed SS by the ISI, was going to be the man on the job. A tried-and-tested sharp-shooter, ex-police officer of Jammu and Kashmir. They had all the details and had already set up the team that was going to tackle him but the details of the operation were unknown. Considering that Ghulam Ali was the best sniper they had and a proven one, it would probably be one single shot from a hidden place. The NSA asked to be kept in the loop constantly as they went about the operation.

The NSA informed and briefed the prime minister and tried to persuade him to call off the inauguration or postpone it. But the prime minister was adamant. He was going to do it. It would be a great gesture opening up the direct road called the Kartarpur Corridor that would connect the holiest of the Sikh shrines, Darbar Sahib Kartarpur in Pakistan, associated with Guru Nanak, the first guru of the Sikhs, to Dera Baba Nanak in the Punjab, India, where the guru had spent a long time.

'It's your business to ensure security,' said the PM, 'and my business to do what is good for the nation.'

Ghulam Ali was a loner. He was a tall and fair with brown eyes and a flowing beard. Wearing a turban he disguised himself as a Sikh pilgrim and as planned he crossed the border with other pilgrims using a false passport provided by the ISI.

One month ago he had, with the help of the ISI, acquired the weapon of his choice, the Russian Lobaev sniper rifle SVLK–14S with a 408 CheyTac calibre and a muscle velocity of 900 m/s. With a 10.3mm/D30 bullet and a powerful precision scope fitted on the top it weighed 9.5 kg and had a maximum firing range of 2300 metres.

It took him and a Russian arms specialist about a week to figure out how to dismantle it piece by piece and reassemble it. In ten to fifteen days he was shooting even a moving target perfectly at the Balakot firing range at 1500 yards.

Ghulam Ali loved the weapon. Its precision, the minimum recoil and the muffled sound of the shot as he pulled the trigger.

Agents of the Khalistan Movement helped him carry the dismantled parts of the gun piece by piece across the border.

He reached Dera Baba Nanak one week in advance, disguised as a Sikh. He checked himself into Hotel Guru Kripa barely three-and-a-half km from the Bara Bhai Darbar border under the name provided in the passport, 'Sukwinder Singh'. It was the gate on the Indian side of the border that was going to be inaugurated by the prime minister.

Ghulam Ali would assemble the weapon on the day of the event as the parts would be handed over to him on the previous evening. It would take him half an hour to assemble the gun.

He had recced the area and the best place to fix the gun would be the ventilator of his bathroom which faced the border. His room was on the sixth and top floor which provided a clear view.

Not a lot of big trees, only green fields. There was nothing that would come in the way.

The pandal for the inauguration had already been put up 100 metres from the cast-iron border gate. Men from the police, intelligence agencies, the BSF and the CRPF had already started combing the area and hotels were being checked. His room, the Sikh manager informed him, had also been checked when he had gone out. 'Routine,' he had said. 'All the rooms were checked.' Ghulam Ali had nothing to worry about. The parts would be in his room after two days. He had information that they had already crossed the border. He switched off his phone and threw it into a nearby well as he went for a walk in the evening. RAW would be trying to trace his calls.

* * *

It was all in the newspapers. The Indian prime minister would arrive at the Sri Guru Ram Dass Jee International Airport forty-two km away and would drive down with his motorcade to the site of the inauguration on Sunday, 15 April, which was also Guru Nanak's birthday.

First he would meet with the local party leaders and functionaries of the Sikh religious organizations and other prominent people at the pandal. Then the chief minister of Punjab would hand over the remote control gadget for opening the gates 100 meters away. The gates would be opened at precisely 1.00 p.m. after which the national anthem would be played by the military band.

The function would end and the prime minister would drive back to the airport. Ghulam Ali had to choose the right time and opportunity to shoot. He had to finish the operation with just one shot, no more, and escape.

* * *

On the day of the event, the NSA got a call from at 6 a.m. 'Sir, it looks like SS has crossed the border but we haven't found any reliable clues. We are yet to get information from our agents. All the hotels around have been searched but nothing has been found. We are keeping a close watch. The armed and paramilitary forces have been alerted for maximum security. We'll find him, sir, but let's us not take a risk.'

'Over,' said the NSA. 'We have directed the bodyguards to form an almost impenetrable shield. Vande Mataram.'

'Vande Mataram, sir.'

* * *

At 12.00 p.m. am on the same day, Ghulam Ali set up his Lobaev Sniper rifle on the tripod with the barrel pointing through the bathroom ventilator. He had opened the glass pane just enough to get clearance for the barrel. From the outside, it was hardly visible.

He looked through the scope and adjusted it to get a clear view of the stage. He would know exactly where the prime minister would be standing only when the event started. At the moment, he focused at the centre of the stage.

Then he shut the door of the bathroom, came into the bedroom and prayed a few *rakaats* of namaaz. The loudspeaker had started announcing the arrival of the prime minister. He would be on the stage in half an hour or so. He went back to the bathroom, shut the door and looked through the ventilator. The cavalcade was still not in sight. The chief minister and other VIPs were already on the stage. The chief minister seemed to have arrived with his extended family. There were several women and three or four kids on stage, waving the national flag.

At ten minutes to 1.00 the cavalcade came in sight. The security forces came out first and surrounded the prime minister's armoured Land Rover. The prime minister and the armed security men driving with him got out and walked to the stage.

The chief minister greeted the prime minister and his wife handed the PM a bouquet of roses which one of the plain-clothed men took from him.

Ghulam Ali looked through the scope and focused on his target. He knew the PM would be wearing a bulletproof vest. He needed a clear view of his head. The bullet had to go through the right temple and out through the left. It had to be just one shot and he had to do it quickly. Something told him the RAW sharp shooters would find him soon. He had to do it now.

Ghulam Ali lifted the pendant he always wore on his neck and flipped it open. Huma smiled back at him from the photograph; brown hair, blue eyes, sparkling teeth. He was going to win the war against the killers of his daughter.

The security man, who had till then blocked the view of the PM's head, moved aside. Now was the time. He focused on the right temple. His index finger was on the trigger. And then something most unexpected happened.

The PM bent down and picked up a little child, probably from the chief minister's family, and held her close to him, smiling and saying something. The little girl's head now hid the side of his head. He had to shoot both.

He focused the scope on the girl's head. She turned and looked in the direction of the gun and . . . laughed. Ghulam Ali froze. His hands went cold and his finger refused to pull the trigger. It was Huma, his darling daughter; the brown hair, the chubby cheeks, the blue eyes, the white pearly teeth . . . No, it couldn't be true. Huma was dead. She had been shot in front of him. No, not possible. But he missed the chance and couldn't get to pull the trigger on time.

Right then, the bathroom door burst open. The Special Section commandos had AK-47s. There were four of them. 'Raise your hands and don't move. We have you covered.'

Ghulam Ali knew it was the end. How did they know? Probably had an informer among the Khalistanis. It was time. He put his right hand into his pocket to get at the deadly cyanide capsule that would take his life in no time and transport his soul to heaven.

The commandos took no risk. They thought he was trying to get his pistol and shot him dead.

The prime minister put the child down, pressed the remote control and the opening ceremony was over. The black cats spoke on wireless phones and one of them whispered to the PM.

He was quickly taken to the car and whisked away.

By evening, news channels were going crazy about the attempted assassination by a terrorist, backed and fully orchestrated by the ISI. The debates started, one louder than the other. Soon all the channels were agog with the news.

The little baby who would have died along with the prime minister if the shot had been fired was the chief minister's granddaughter.

No one knew that it was Ghulam Ali's love for his daughter that had saved the prime minister and the little one's life.

A Comanche Episode

25 November 1864

The blazing Texas sun had cooled to a pleasant orange shade and was beginning to set among the wild oaks in the south bend of the Brazos River, Young County.

The battle was over. The white men had been routed. Their soldiers had retreated to Fort Belknap, but many Comanche warriors had died too and a small band led by their medicine man, Pale Coyote, came searching among the dead bodies for Chief White Eagle.

Severely wounded and bleeding heavily, he saw them coming through half-closed eyes. He knew he would die soon, but they wouldn't let him die in peace when they found him. A chief couldn't be buried without the terrible funeral ritual.

They found him. The medicine man went on his knees, put his ear near his throat and declared, 'The Great Spirit Manitou has not allowed Chief White Eagle to die. I can hear the death rattle. Let's begin the death ritual before his spirit escapes to join the realm of the spirits. Pick up the chief's body.'

He knew what torture was coming but was too weak to stop it or register a protest. The last torture before the peaceful oblivion of death was near. He wished he had died before they had found him.

The warriors picked up his limp, almost dead, body and carried it to their settlement close to the south end of the Brazos River. They were in a hurry.

'Bring his dead horse, Lightning. There he is,' ordered the medicine man. The warriors picked up the dead horse and followed.

They ran fast carrying the dying chief and his dead horse to their settlement, two miles away. The sun had set and only a faint orange hue suffused the skyline.

All the men, women and children came out of their pyramid-shaped buffalo-hide tepees to welcome them, for this was a solemn occasion.

The burial pit for the chief and his horse which would enable him to ride faster into the realm of spirits had already been dug and made ready.

They laid the rider and the horse side by side and prepared them for the burial. The medicine man put his ears once again to White Eagle's throat and smiled with satisfaction. He was still alive and could hear the rattle of the air struggling to make the final exit. Now they were in a hurry. The body had to be bent into a special posture before death took over and rigor mortis set in. He had to be bundled into a round-ball-like shape before being ritually placed inside the grave.

A loud gurgle came out of Chief White Eagle's mouth as two warriors bent both his legs so that his thighs pressed against his stomach and his knees doubled up near the chest. Then they pulled his arms around his ankles and tied them with a rope. White Eagle felt a wave of searing pain go through his entire body. He had never felt such pain in his life. Then they pulled the head forward to bend his chin to his neck. The vertebrae broke with a cracking sound and he was freed from pain forever. The peace of death took over his soul.

* * *

25 November 2018

Prof. John Hamilton, archeologist and historian, woke up from the deep sleep he had drifted into after the torturous dream of the ritual burial he had to undergo as Chief White Eagle.

The summer sun had already risen high. The clock on the wall showed 9 a.m., later than his usual time to wakeup. Jumping out of bed, he went straight to the writing desk by the window and opened his laptop. He had to write this down before the memory of the dream evaporated. He smiled to himself as he typed. The dream had solved the problem. Now he knew why they hadn't found the Comanche graves. He and his assistants had been looking for the usual rectangular graves. The Comanche bent the dead bodies into almost elliptical shapes and so the graves were probably like circular pits. They needed to look for mounds.

After typing out the entire dream, he went to the washroom and got ready to go out to the site on the southern side of the Brazos River where the excavations were going on.

He microwaved a chocolate croissant, ate a banana, had a cup of black coffee, got out of the house and hopped into the four-wheel drive, grey Wrangler Jeep. The drive to the site would take him about forty-five minutes to an hour across a mud road which became quite treacherous when it rained. But it hadn't rained for quite some days.

As he drove through the oak-and-pecan-tree-lined track, he thought about the dream he had. What amused him was that he had become Chief White Eagle in the dream. It was so real as if, as the Hindus say, he had been the Comanche chief in this 'past life'. He dismissed the thought and began planning the day's work.

Prof. John Hamilton, an alumnus of the University of Texas, Austin, had earned his doctorate from the Texas Archeological Research Laboratory, specializing in Native Indian archaeology with special reference to the Comanche Native Indians.

For reasons unknown, John's interest in the Native Indians, especially the Comanche, was aroused even at the age of seven or eight. His favourite sport was to dress up as an Indian chief, complete with war paint and armed with a bow and arrow, and walk in the woods that surrounded his house in Bull Creek, Austin.

At the university, he had eagerly devoured all the research material of the 1920s of pioneers in Native Indian archaeology like E.B. 'Ted' Sayles and Cyrus N. Ray.

After finishing his studies he had, with help of a generous grant from the Ford Foundation, immediately plunged into an on-site research. At thirty-four, he already had three years of archaeological research to his credit, for the most part in and around the Young County, on both banks of the Brazos River.

A lot of material had been unearthed but they hadn't found a single Comanche ritual burial site. John couldn't help smiling to himself because now he knew where he had gone wrong and what to look for.

* * *

He loved the ranch house that his friend Michael had allowed him to use while he was away in Mexico with his girlfriend. Fifty acres of land with an abundance of oak and pecan trees and the muddy Brazos River flowing on the western boundary.

It was a beautiful house and what he loved best was the master bedroom that Michael let him use. The large French window on one side gave him a grand view of the Brazos River, the grand oak trees and the stables. Of the three horses, he was fond of Silver Star, the white Arabian stallion. The fondness seemed mutual and in one month of his stay at the ranch, he had gone riding at least twenty times. Silver Star seemed almost proud of John Hamilton as he rode around the campus. The only other person around was Marcos the caretaker who also took care of the horses and lived in the outhouse near the stables.

John Hamilton reached the excavation site and stepped out of his car. The workforce consisting of eight local Mexicans and two white men who supervised the work had already arrived. As he walked towards them, John for a fleeting second felt like a native Indian chief walking towards his subjects but to his relief, it passed quickly and he was Prof. John Hamilton once again.

'Hi Peter,' he said to the chief supervisor. 'What's up?'

'Already dug up quite a few areas, but no sign of a ritual burial, John.'

John Hamilton looked around thoughtfully. 'You know what, Peter, I think we are looking in the wrong places for the wrong thing.'

'What do you mean?'

Prof. Hamilton didn't want to reveal the source of his knowledge. It was as if the dream was sacrosanct. He merely said, 'I think we should look for mounds, not rectangular graves.'

Anton was confused but did not want to question the professor. He also remembered he had surveyed the area and there was, in fact, something of a similar nature.

'Okay, I don't get it but just there on the northern slope, there are two circular mounds. Shall we start digging?'

The workers started the excavation. It took them almost the whole day with a short lunch break. Most of the digging was done by hand. Excavators were used minimally for fear of losing valuable historical material. At seven feet, they came across what they were looking for. In one of the graves, they found the remains. A well-preserved skeleton tied up in a fetal posture, with buffalo-hide tapes draped in the same material stitched together. Most of the buffalo hide had turned brittle and fell off when they lifted the skeleton out. It looked like the grave of an important person, perhaps a chief given the eagle feather headdress lying, almost intact, next to the remains.

In the other were the skeletal remains of the horse.

As the mound was being excavated, Anton heard an odd speech. He turned to look where it was coming from and realized it was Prof. Hamilton.

'Can't make out what you are saying, boss,' said Anton, confused. 'Think you need some water. Your voice sounds weird. Too much exposure to Texan sun, I guess.'

Prof. Hamilton woke up from the semi-trance into which he had entered for a minute or two and realized he had been speaking in the ancient Uto–Aztecan Comanche language he had been studying for some time from the Comanche Native Indians who lived in a reservation in Oklahoma.

'Thank you, Anton,' Prof. Hamilton said, drinking the water provided by Anton. 'Yes, I think it's the heat.'

It was getting dark when Prof. Hamilton returned home. He had instructed Peter and Anton to carefully bring the skeletal remains to the ranch house first thing in the morning. One part of the house had been converted into an archaeological laboratory-cum-museum and contained hundreds of artefacts from the diggings. That's where Prof. Hamilton spent most of this time when not doing fieldwork.

Something peculiar was going on for a month since his arrival there. Almost every night he had weird dreams, mostly of Comanche Indians and except for the terribly painful dream he had the previous night, he seemed to enjoy them.

There were dreams of riding into the battlefield, fighting the Tonkawa tribe and the White men, of ritual dances and offering of sacrifice to the Great Spirit Manitou, colourful pow wows and ritual smoking of the peace pipe prepared by the medicine man. It was as if the history and anthropology of the Comanches were being played out to him in dream sequences. He was the Comanche Chief White Eagle in most of the dreams and in a way enjoyed them though the only part he was horrified with was the occasional ritual cannibalism of their enemies, the Tonkawas. When this happened, he would wake up from the sleep and remain awake till the sun came up.

Marcos the caretaker had cooked him a good meal of wild boar and buffalo ribs. He had a glass of Chardonnay from Michael's cellar. He was feeling tired after a whole day out and decided to sleep early.

With his reading lamp on, he read *Empire of the Summer Moon: Quanah Parker and the Rise and Fall of the Comanches, the Most Powerful Indian Tribe in American History* by S.C. Gwynne for hardly ten minutes when sleep overpowered him. He switched off the lamp and fell asleep.

* * *

Full moon night, 1868

Chief White Eagle rode up to the sacred sacrificial fire pit on his white steed, Lightning. It was a full moon night. The elders of the tribe had gathered around with their faces painted for the pow wow. Pale Coyote, the medicine man, was already there.

The sacrificial offering was a buffalo which was tied near the pit. White Eagle with his eagle-feather headdress and buffalo-hide cloak sat on the spiritual seat.

The pow wow dance began around the fire pit. Pale Coyote chanted the incantations and threw herbs into the fire. The warriors chanted praise to Manitou the Great Spirit and the gods of the river, mountains and forest.

With a whistle, the medicine man stopped the ceremonial dance. He and Chief White Eagle had plucked the datura fruit in the early part of the moonlit night. Pale Coyote had powdered the seeds and mixed them with tobacco to be smoked in the buffalo-horn peace pipe. A small portion of the powder was mixed with heated buffalo milk. This would be taken only by the chief, the medicine man and the warriors who would behead the buffalo with one stroke of their axes from either side.

The warriors untied the buffalo. As it came charging, they struck with their axes with great precision. The buffalo was beheaded in a flash. The blood that gushed was collected in a dried gourd bowl and poured over the sacrificial fire.

As the flames blazed, the air was filled with the fumes of burning blood. The body and head of the buffalo were removed and taken to the community hearth to be cooked.

The medicine man lit the peace pipe filled with tobacco, laced with the powder of the datura seeds and after three puffs, passed it on to the chief. White Eagle took three puffs and passed it. All the warriors smoked, passing it to each other.

After a few minutes, Pale Coyote gave the signal for the dance to resume. The warriors danced around fire, with their tomahawks invoking the gods with loud cries like wild animals.

White Eagle went into a trance. In his astral body, he travelled to the spirit realms and reached the dwelling of the

Great Spirit, Manitou. Manitou spoke in a thundering voice from behind a big oak tree. 'White Eagle, you shall be born after countless years as a pale-faced, white man. Find the datura and smoke the peace pipe to come back to me.'

The year 2018

The thunder woke Prof. John Hamilton from his strange and almost frightening dream. It was raining outside with flashes of lightning and loud thunder, the first rain after summer. It was daybreak. Hamilton woke up wondering if the rain would stop and he could continue his outdoor work.

When Peter and Anton came at 8.00 a.m. in their blue Jeep Wrangler to deposit the artefacts in the lab, the rain had almost stopped.

The summer had been so hot that all the water was absorbed by the dry earth. It didn't look like it had rained. There weren't even small puddles anywhere.

'Shift the excavation team to the clearing which is down the ravines on the left of the house,' he said to Peter. 'It's just a fifteen-minutes walk from here, a little away from the flood plains of the river. From the gate, there is a straight mud road that leads there,' John added knowingly.

He continued, 'When you guys arrive, I'll be at the gate. The road is rocky and uneven so we'll have to drive carefully.'

'Okay,' said Peter. 'It will take us about an hour to get there.'

'Sure, will wait,' John said, surprised by the certainty with which he had described the location. He had never been there before.

John Hamilton had a quick breakfast, his usual croissants, fried eggs and coffee, and climbed down the rocky ravine from the northern side of the ranch house. He was taking a short cut to an unknown place. It was kind of tricky but he managed to reach the clearing in the centre of the ravine.

It was exactly as he had seen in the dream. He then found the rocky mud road leading to the gate. He walked up the path. It took him three quarters of an hour to reach the gate.

He looked at the watch. The team would probably arrive in fifteen minutes. He looked at the Rolex Oyster Perpetual, a watch Nina had gifted him. It took him back to the time he had been a student at the Texas Archeological Research Laboratory, and had fallen in love with her, the pretty, doe-eyed dark-haired research scholar whose father was a Texan oil tycoon. They were deeply in love until a fatal car accident snatched her away one month before she was to get her PhD. For three months, he suffered the trauma and needed psychiatric attention. It was then that the dreams had started.

In the dreams, he was the Comanche Chief White Eagle and his squaw was Nina (Sweet Dove) who was kidnapped by the Tonkawa tribe. It took him about a year to get out of depression though he continued with a mild dose of medication.

The team arrived in two trucks and two pick-ups. John Hamilton jumped into the Nissan pick-up driven by Anton and in ten minutes, they were at the clearing.

Hamilton marked the sites to be excavated and sat down on a folding chair to watch over the work. Fifteen people and the two supervisors started their work.

Hamilton got up and walked towards the river. In the dream, he had clearly seen Pale Coyote pluck the datura fruit from a dense thicket not too far from the clearing. In ten minutes, John Hamilton found what he was looking for. The datura, also known as devil's weed, with its white trumpet-shaped flowers. Quickly he plucked three of the fruits, the thorn apples and put them into the pockets of his dungarees and quietly walked back to the site.

By noon, they had discovered the fire pit and the skeletal remains of the sacrificial animal, the buffalo. There were also a number of roughly hewn stone cups and the large peace pipes fashioned out of buffalo horn.

Suddenly, it started raining heavily. The rainy season had set in. They wound up the excavations for the day, dropped Prof. Hamilton at the ranch house and deposited the artefacts in the lab.

'We'll see how it goes,' said Prof. Hamilton. 'If the rain stops, we'll start in the morning tomorrow. You guys call it a day and go have a good time.'

He paid them their wages, gave them a big bonus and said goodbye.

He carefully placed the thorn apples in a glass bowl on the bedside table, changed into his pyjamas and had a lovely lunch of beef steak and potatoes cooked by Marcos.

Marcos also found him a bottle of Walt Bob's Ranch Chardonnay. He had two glasses of the excellent wine.

After lunch, he felt sleepy which was unusual for him. 'All right, let me take a short siesta,' he said to himself. When he woke up he planned to check the Internet to see if there was anything on preparing a peace pipe and the use of the datura extract. He fell into a deep sleep and had a vivid dream.

Pale Coyote was teaching him to how to prepare the peace pipe and also the method of using the datura seeds.

When he woke up, it was already seven in the evening. He made himself a cup of coffee and went out to sit on the old rocking chair that stood on the deck. On a pad with a pencil, he noted down the details of his dream.

The rain had stopped. The sky was clear. The full moon was shining, cool and bright. A strange peace entered his heart. He rocked himself for a long time.

Marcos came up and asked him if he could rustle up some dinner for him.

'Not really,' said Prof. Hamilton. 'I'm not hungry. Just give me a glass of the excellent Chardonnay you gave me at lunch and perhaps some potato chips.'

Marcos placed the wine and chips beside him on a side table, and said goodnight.

'Is there some milk in the fridge?'

'Yes, sir.'

'Goodnight again. See you in the morning.'

A plan unfolded in Prof. Hamilton's mind. He finished his wine and chips. The night was getting chilly so he shifted indoors and sat on the sofa, going through the plan in detail.

The first thing was to prepare the peace pipe and the datura seed infusion. Michael had several packets of tobacco he used for his pipe that were in the drawer of the big writing table in the library. There was milk in the fridge and he had seen a small stone mortar and pestle in the kitchen. All the things needed were there, ready for him to use. No hassles.

Prof. Hamilton finished his wine and went into the kitchen. First he cut the thorn apple and carefully removed the tiny grey seeds. In all he could get around twenty seeds. Adding a little milk from the fridge, he ground into a thick paste, using the mortar and pestle. He mixed the paste thoroughly in a ceramic bowl with warmed-up buffalo's milk until it acquired a uniform consistency that could be drank smoothly.

Then he poured most of the datura-dissolved milk into a clean bottle, corked it tight and put it into his leather shoulder bag. Some of the infusion, he left in the bowl to be mixed with the tobacco.

Next, he set about preparing the peace pipe. First he washed the buffalo-horn pipe clean and wiped it dry. Then he opened two packets of the Cavenders tobacco and placed their content in a shallow soup bowl.

Sprinkling the leftover datura infusion in the ceramic bowl into the tobacco, he mixed it thoroughly. The tobacco smelt good. He placed the datura-infused tobacco under the fan in the living room for ten minutes to dry and went into the laboratory to change into the buffalo-hide robe worn by Comanche chiefs which he had acquired from the local native Indian store. He had also bought some stone bead necklaces, deer-skin moccasins and an eagle-feather headdress worn by the warriors. He put these on as well and adjusted the headdress. As he dressed, it occurred to him that the preparation had happened so naturally. It was as if he had done all this before and knew how to go about it.

He stuffed the buffalo-horn pipe, the tobacco which was now in a plastic pouch and a box of matches into the same bag in which he had placed the sacred milk.

He took a look at the dressing-table mirror in the bedroom. He looked every inch a Comanche chief. He slung the leather bag containing the stuff across his left shoulder and stepped out into the chill moonlit night. Now came the tricky part. He needed to take Silver Star out of the stable without waking up the sleeping Marcos whose outhouse was close to the stable.

To his surprise, Silver Star obeyed his almost whispered instructions and walked out without even a neigh.

He mounted Silver Star and rode out to the sacred ritual grounds down the ravine. He spoke to Silver Star—now Lightning—in the Comanche tongue, 'Steady, Lightning, careful, let's go to the sacred grounds.'

He dismounted form the horse, tied it to an oak tree and taking his shoulder bag, walked over to an almost flat-surfaced boulder. It was in the northern side of the excavated fire pit. That's when he discovered, to his surprise, that the embers in the fire pit were still hot and glowing.

Sitting down at one end of the boulder's surface, facing the fire pit, he unpacked the bag and placed the required materials on his right.

There seemed to be nobody in sight but he could hear the ritual chant coming from the surrounding oak grove. The voices were muffled.

He opened the bottle of the sacred milk and drank it up at one go. It was bitter. Then he prepared the peace pipe by filling it with the already prepared sacred tobacco. He successfully lit the pipe and sitting cross-legged, smoked. John—now White Eagle—allowed the peace to enter his soul as the smoke filled his lungs.

By then, the sound of the chanting had become louder. It filled the air. Many voices spoke together. A burning sensation came upon his body as if it was set on fire. He saw that the glowing embers in the fire pit had broken into flames. Tongues of fire leapt up in the pit.

Suddenly, one voice among the many spoke loud and clear. 'I am Manitou, the Great Spirit, your father. We sent you down on earth to be born as a paleface white man to reveal the history of the Comanches and our great ways to the world. Come back to us now. Sweet Dove is waiting for you—Cross the Brazos, the river god also beckons you, come.'

The chanting now rose to a crescendo. '*Kana makki— hallu hallu—pakchi tilla mooka sira sira.*'

(Come, come. We wait for you, slowly cross the river. Doe Eye is waiting. Manitou commands.)

The oak trees were suffused with a weird orange glow. Chief White Eagle mounted his steed Lightning and rode into the Brazos River. He could clearly see Doe Eye beckoning from the clouded sky. It started raining heavily. A heavy thunderstorm. In a freak, flash flood, the Brazos River claimed Chief White Eagle and his steed, Lightning.

* * *

Several days after Marcos reported the mysterious disappearance of Prof. John Hamilton and the horse to the sheriff of Young County his body was recovered many miles away on the eastern banks of the Brazos River. The horse's body was never recovered. The post-mortem report said that he had died of an overdose of datura stramonium, the Devil's snare, a hallucinogenic plant which, above a certain dose, is known to be fatal. This was the only death reported by datura poisoning in Young County area.

* * *

Prof. John Hamilton's notebooks and his laptop yielded rich and comprehensive material on the history and anthropology of the Comanche Native Indians and went on to become the major research source for students of Native Indian Studies. Prof. John Hamilton had recorded the material under the pen name of Chief White Eagle and his Email ID was whiteeagle.comanche@gmail.com.

The Strange Case of Mastan

This happened not so long ago.

On the outskirts of Singarcoil, a small town in Tamil Nadu, lived Mastan bhai, a butcher who had inherited his trade from his father.

There were two other Muslim butchers who sold halal mutton—halal being similar to the kosher meat of the Jews, a religiously sanctioned way of slaughtering the animal by cutting its carotid artery and windpipe, so that most of the blood spurted out before the animal died—but most people preferred Mastan's mutton. Somehow it was tastier, tender and always fresh, though a little costlier.

Even on busy days like Sundays, holidays and festivals like Ramadan and Bakra-Eid, Mastan worked alone. He didn't believe in hiring assistants. He was a widower; his wife had died childless ten years ago. He didn't want to marry again even though remarriage was not frowned upon in his religion.

Among the Muslim community he was considered an odd man because celibacy was not a religiously sanctioned mode of life. He lived alone, cooked his own food and had cut himself off from all his relatives.

He was not a very religious man and hardly visited the mosque for prayers. The mufti of the mosque tried to persuade him to attend prayers but left him alone after a while. Considering Mastan's wrestler-like body, stern face and the fact that he was a butcher, the mufti decided to choose the principle of non-interference. No one questioned his religious beliefs or bothered him any more.

Mastan's idea of religion was that it was a sham. His community would have been shocked if they had heard this.

Not that he was a practising Muslim, but he had turned into a complete atheist after his dear wife's death. No prayers had saved her. After that, he questioned all religious beliefs, including the one that on doomsday, the day of reckoning, when the world would end, all dead bodies would be brought to life, would rise from their graves at God's call to answer for their deeds and would be sent to heaven or hell according to their actions.

He had seen a TV channel on religious beliefs of the Parsis and appreciated the fact that even dead bodies were put to good use and fed to the vultures. He didn't even believe that halal meat was in anyway better than non-halal meat or that it was a sin to eat pork or meat that was not sanctioned by the scriptures but he kept his beliefs to himself for fear of being excommunicated. As far as he was concerned, it was enough to be outwardly a part of the community as long as it helped him continue with his trade of being a butcher and running a profitable business of selling so-called halal meat. He kept the real reason why the meat he sold was tastier a secret. All that mattered was that there was great demand for his meat and that his business was growing so fast that he could replace his bike with a Maruti 800 and buy a bigger fridge.

And so life continued for Mastan and quite profitably so, or so he thought.

Two other butchers of Singarcoil, Karim and Irfan, met at a teashop one Friday to discuss among other matters the question of how Mastan was doing so much better than them and why many customers thought his mutton tasted better.

'I suspect he is adding beef or something else to the mutton secretly,' said Irfan. 'You know, he recently got a big new fridge, perhaps he keeps some secret ingredient in it.'

'I don't know,' said Karim. 'But there is something funny going on. You know, he hardly comes to the mosque for prayer but the other day, Tangayya, the goldsmith who is his neighbour told me he saw Mastan drive towards the mosque near the graveyard at around 2.30 at night last week and return in two hours. When he casually questioned him he said he had gone to the mosque for some kind of special prayers at night.

But the mosque is closed at night. The muezzin opens the mosque only at 4.30 for the prayer call. When I told Tangayya about this he said he didn't know but this is what Mastan told him.'

'That's strange,' said Irfan. 'So, what do you think he was up to?'

Karim said, 'Do you think he is practising some kind of black magic in the graveyard to improve his business? I think it's worth keeping a watch at night and perhaps follow him discreetly next time he ventures out on his nocturnal adventure. If he really is doing something like that, it's against Islam. We have to tell the mufti and he needs to be excommunicated and thrown out of here.'

'I have asked Tangayya to alert us next time he sees something happening.'

'Okay, let's see,' said Irfan and they went back home on their motorbikes.

A week later, at 2.30 a.m., Karim was woken up by a call from Tangayya. 'Karim bhai, our friend just drove out of his house in the direction of the graveyard. If you hurry up we can investigate. I don't want to go alone. Who knows what he's up to?'

'Okay, I am game,' said Karim. 'Will be there in five minutes.'

Karim didn't want to call Irfan and disturb him at this time. He got on his Suzuki motorcycle and rode towards Tangayya's house.

Tangayya was waiting outside. He climbed on to the pillion and they rode in the direction of the graveyard. When they reached the old mosque that was close to the graveyard, they found Mastan's Maruti 800 parked there by the side of the road.

They parked the bike near the mosque and walked to the car. All the doors seemed locked but the hatchback boot was open. They opened it up and looked in. There was nothing inside. 'The mosque is closed. Let's check the graveyard,' whispered Karim.

Carefully, making as little noise as possible, they entered the graveyard through the northern gate. Instead of a pleasant feeling, the heady fragrance of the jasmine creeper someone had planted in the graveyard gave them the creeps. 'Female ghosts are supposed to smell of jasmine,' whispered Tangayya with a shiver.

Just then an owlet screeched somewhere and Karim's heart missed a beat. 'Do you have a flashlight?'

'I have one,' said Tangayya. 'But let's use it only if necessary. Mastan might see the light and get alerted.'

Just then, the clouds moved and the half-moon made an appearance.

'Superb! Now we have some light,' said Karim. 'But I don't see him anywhere.'

Then they heard what sounded like someone digging, the sound of a pickaxe and spade.

On the southern side of the graveyard was an old tomb of an unknown saint, now in ruins, with a simple, rectangular mausoleum built around it. The sound seemed to be coming from that direction.

'Let's go and hide behind the tomb and see what's going on,' said Karim.

They crept towards the mausoleum and saw Mastan with a spade, removing the earth from a fairly large pit and throwing it on the sides.

'I think he is digging for treasure,' said Tangayya.

'No,' whispered Karim, 'I don't understand . . . This is horrible. He is digging up the new grave of Abdullah's fifteen-year-old daughter Salima who died in a freak accident. She fell from the swing, hit her head on a tree trunk and died instantly of a head injury. She was buried only yesterday.'

'I think he has gone crazy. We should stop him right now.'

'Wait,' said Tangayya. 'Let's see what he's up to. It's too macabre to think about but I have a faint idea of what he is trying to do. Let's wait and catch him red-handed.'

'All right,' said Karim, keeping his emotions under control.

For one hour they waited with bated breath. When Mastan brought out the cloth-wrapped body, laid it on the side and tore open the white cloth, Karim could not take it any more. 'I have to stop him!' he whispered to Tangayya.

'No,' said Tangayya. 'We haven't seen the whole drama yet. Please, Karim, let's see what he does. We need to let him complete his task and then catch him at it.'

With great effort, Karim controlled himself and watched Mastan at work

In great haste, Mastan covered the now empty grave and patted the mud into place till it looked just as it had before he had started digging. The rain had softened the earth, making his task easier. Then he looked around to make sure he was alone and, lifting the body of young Salima, walked across the graveyard to his car which was parked near the mosque.

They followed at a discreet distance, careful not to be seen. Crouched behind the northern wall of the mosque they saw with great astonishment Mastan placing Salima's dead body in the boot of his car and pulling the hatchback shut.

Then he got into the driver's seat, started the car and drove away in the direction of his house.

'Now what?' said Karim.

'Let's wait for a while and follow him to his house. If we go after him right now, he will hear the motorcycle.'

A few impatient minutes after the car had gone out of sight, they got on the bike and rode towards Mastan's house. They found his car parked outside the small gate that opened into his backyard. By then, it was almost daylight. Parking the motorcycle near Tangayya's house, they walked to the car and took a look. It was locked and empty.

Karim said, 'I am going to climb the wall and try looking through the window.'

'I'll come too,' said Tangayya. Making as little noise as possible, they climbed the short compound wall and landed on the other side.

From a room at the back end of the house, they heard the sound of a meat-cleaver being used on the wooden butcher's block.

'He is using the cleaver to cut the meat,' said Karim, utterly disgusted. They edged close to the window. The panes were solid teak wood.

'If the panes are not bolted or latched,' whispered Tangayya, 'I'll try to pry one of the panes open.'

'Why don't we break the door open and surprise him?' said Karim.

'If what I think is what he is up to, this is a police case,' said Tangayya. 'There is also a chance of him attacking us. The fellow is a lunatic.'

Tangayya pulled out a pen-knife from his trouser pocket. Pushing the blade into the very narrow space between the corner of one of the window panes and the old wooden frame, he tried to pry it open as noiselessly as possible, hoping that Mastan, intent on whatever he was doing wouldn't hear the sound.

Luck was on their side. The window pane opened a wee bit with a small squeak. The latch had loosened with age.

Tangayya closed one eye and looked through the small opening. The room was well lit with a fluorescent light. The smell of flesh assailed his nostrils. 'Oh, God!' he gasped and, running to the bushes near the compound wall, crouched and threw up.

It was Karim's turn now, and the gruesome sight he saw was more horrifying than anything he could have imagined.

Near the wall was a long wooden table. Young Salima's naked torso minus the head, hands and feet lay on the table. As Karim watched, Mastan chopped off her right leg waist downwards and placed it on the butcher's block which stood in front of the table. He then proceeded to cut it into three or four pieces.

Karim, a hardened butcher though he was, couldn't bear to look any longer.

His instinct was to break the door and confront Mastan but Tangayya, who by then had recovered his composure and was by his side, stopped him.

'First let's get out of here before we are discovered,' said Tangayya. 'I have a strategy which will nail the fellow. It's better the police is involved. Calm down, Karim. My cousin, Perumal, is the inspector in charge of the Singarcoil Police Station. It's too early for him to reach the station but let's go to his house as quickly as possible and tell him.'

Leaving Mastan's house behind, Karim started his motorcycle and they rode to Perumal's house, which was two kilometres away, as fast as they could.

Perumal was getting ready to go to the station and was already in his uniform. He ushered them in, insisted they have a cup of coffee and then heard them out.

'This is shocking!' said Perumal. 'But digging a grave is not considered a major offence and he may get away with a minor punishment. What we can charge him with is food adulteration. The Food Safety and Standards Authority of India has recommended life imprisonment and penalty of ten lakhs for adulterating food products.

'The court is sure to take a serious view of his adulterating goat's meat with, of all things, human flesh taken from newly buried bodies! He will most probably get a life sentence.

'But first we need proof and as quickly as possible. I'll request for an arrest warrant which will take some time but let's go raid the premises and catch him before he cleans up. Let's go.'

Perumal rang up three constables and told them where to come and, taking Tangayya with him, drove down in the police jeep. Karim followed on his bike. On the way, he rang up Irfan on his mobile and gave him a brief description of what was happening.

'He can't just be given a life sentence,' said Irfan, remorsefully. 'He needs to die. I think he should be punished with death as, according to the Quran, dead bodies have to rise and answer Allah on the Day of Judgement. The whole body has to rise. Dead bodies cannot be desecrated and mutilated! They have to face Allah. What Mastan did is against Islam's law and death should be his penalty.'

Karim said, 'I agree with you but we can't take the law in our hands. Anyway, let's see what happens now. You can come and join us at Mastan's house in ten or fifteen minutes. The first step for now is that he should be arrested.'

'I'll see you and this infidel Mastan,' said Irfan, the hatred in his voice unmistakable.

* * *

Inspector Perumal, Tangayya, the three constables and Karim reached Mastan's house. They parked their vehicles, walked in through the gate which was open and went around to the back door.

Inspector Perumal upholstered his revolver and held it in his right hand.

'Open the door, Mastan, or we might have to break the door open.'

For a few minutes there was silence and then the door opened. Mastan, taken by surprise, stood there with the meat cleaver in his right hand.

Everyone froze for a few seconds and then they heard Mastan saying, 'Come in, come in, you don't have to use force.'

Inspector Perumal entered first followed by the policemen, Tangayya and Karim.

The room was well lit by fluorescent bulbs and the smell of bare flesh assailed their nostrils. Tangayya thought he was going to throw up again but managed to control himself.

On the butcher's block were pieces of meat cut into a certain size. A big aluminum basin was kept on a stool.

But what caught everyone's attention were several large cloth bundles placed on the large wooden table in front of the butcher's block.

Inspector Perumal untied one of the cloth bundles and recoiled in shock. Inside was the head of a young girl and two hands.

Recovering from the shock, he undid the other bundles. There were legs and intestines and other assorted parts of a human body.

One of the policemen took photographs.

Two more people entered through the open doors, Irfan, Karim's friend and Abdullah, Salima's father.

The first thing Abdullah saw was his dead daughter Salima's severed head lying on the wooden table.

Utterly in shock, he screamed and started weeping loudly, his whole body shaking. Irfan held his arms and tried to console him.

Perumal threw open the new refrigerator. It was filled with more meat. He then turned to Mastan who had put the meat cleaver on the block and was sitting in a plastic chair with a blank expression on his face.

'So what have you got to say?' Perumal asked in disgust.

Mastan's face broke into a horrible grin. 'I just used the dead body without wasting it,' he said. 'Why waste good, tender meat. I don't believe God is going to call up dead people from the grave. There is no God. All of that is bunkum.

'I first tried this with my wife's body. It's like donating organs for other people's use when someone dies,' Mastan went on with no remorse.

'Human meat is tasty. I meant no dishonour. Why waste precious meat and give it to maggots and worms. Idi Amin of Africa ate human meat. And it is surely tasty when mixed with mutton. Ask my customers. They bought meat from me because it was tasty.'

None of the people standing there could believe their ears.

Perumal said in disgust, 'I think this fellow has gone completely crazy. Don't know if the judge will send him to a mental hospital or jail.

'Pick up some pieces of the meat and put it in a ziplock bag,' Inspector Perumal ordered one of the constables. 'We need to send it to the forensic lab. As for this fellow, handcuff him. We will take him into custody.'

It was then that something that no one expected happened.

Abdullah, who seemed to have been frozen at the the gruesome sight of his daughter's remains, suddenly turned towards Mastan. With one swift leap, he snatched the meat cleaver lying on the butcher's block. Screaming, 'Pig! Non-believer! *Kafir*, enemy of Islam!', he sprang on Mastan and cleaved his neck and throat with one swift stroke.

Mastan fell off the chair, blood spurting from his throat.

The body convulsed for a moment and then lay still.

Abdullah threw away the cleaver and surrendered to Inspector Perumal who was holding his revolver with the barrel turned in his direction.

'Sir, you can arrest me for murder. But I think by killing this infidel, I have done a glorious deed in Allah's eyes. When I die I will be given a place in paradise, Allah is my witness. The angels shall declare me a martyr.'

Strangely, Abdullah was smiling and quite composed.

'Handcuff this man—Abdullah,' said Inspector Perumal, 'and take him into custody. Call for an ambulance.'

While waiting for the ambulance, Perumal bent down and examined Mastan's pulse and heartbeat. He knew he was dead.

* * *

When the case came up in the magistrate's court, Abdullah was given the death sentence. Abdullah accepted the judgment without any emotion. As he was led away he was seen whispering a prayer.

The media called it the 'The Graveyard Mastan Case.'

Different people reacted differently to the case. There were even some who insisted that Mastan's mutton had been the tastiest mutton they ever had in their lives. They were not bothered by what he mixed it with to enhance the taste.

Acknowledgements

I would like to acknowledge Ernest Hemingway, whose works inspired me to state facts directly and not exaggerate too much, and Lakshmi Kumar for typing my scribbles with great care and accuracy.